A SAMPLING OF MURDER

EMILY JAMES

STRONGHOLD BOOKS

Editor: Christopher Saylor at www.saylorediting.wordpress.com/services/

Cover Design: Mariah Sinclair at www.mariahsinclair.com

Published February 2021 by Stronghold Books

Ebook ISBN 978-1-988480-25-1; Print Book ISBN 978-1-988480-26-8

ALSO BY EMILY JAMES

Maple Syrup Mysteries

Cupcake Truck Mysteries

FREE TIPS FOR AMAZING CUPCAKES

Each book in the Cupcake Truck Mysteries includes a cupcake recipe, but even when you have a great recipe, baking the perfect cupcake can sometimes be hard.

To receive the top 10 tips for amazing cupcakes (inspired by the Cupcake Truck Mysteries sleuth, Isabel), sign up for my newsletter at www.subscribepage.com/cupcakes.

(If you're already a member of my newsletter, no need to worry. I've emailed you a link to the tips too!)

From the moment I heard it, I'd had a bad feeling about the unconventional way my business partner Claire had arranged for us to rent a physical storefront. But the insurance money I'd received from my burned-out food truck wasn't going to be enough to both let us start a physical location and also buy a tiny food truck that we could use for events. Not without resorting to some unusual ideas.

I flipped through the pages of the contract Claire had negotiated. Even after reading it multiple times, it still all looked like I was trying to read a foreign language. One so different from English that the letters weren't even the same. I'd never thought I was stupid, but I'd never gone to college either, and the legalese made me feel like I shouldn't have even graduated from primary school, let alone junior high.

"Walk me through the idea slowly," I said. "One more time."

Listening to Claire was the least I could do after she'd spent so much time negotiating this deal for us after we found our dream location. A dream location that was well out of our price range for a rental property.

"In a nutshell, the owner's willing to give us a break on the rent so we can afford the place." She planted her hands on her hips. "In exchange for a percentage of the business."

Because I'd been hiding from my husband since I'd originally run away, I'd incorporated my business from the start. That had allowed me to have a bank account even though I wasn't using my real name.

We could technically sell or trade off some of the business as we wished.

Doing it just felt like selling one of my kidneys in order to pay for a heart transplant. While I might not need two kidneys to survive, it was still a piece of me. It'd been hard enough taking on Claire as a business partner, and she and I were the closet thing I had to family. Her, her cousin Dan, and his adopted daughter Janie were.

"A small percentage," Claire said. "Page two, at the bottom."

My expression must have given away my reticence. "What if we want to change locations in the future?"

"Page five. If we have to leave the location for a legitimate reason—"

I opened my mouth to point out that language was vague and could come back to hurt us later.

Claire held up her hand. "There's a list outlining the valid reasons. If we have to leave for any legitimate reason, his share of the business goes down to a nominal amount. Just enough for him to recoup the lost rent over the course of a few years. If he dies within the first year, his share of the business immediately reverts to us rather than passing to his next of kin since we won't have gotten enough return on the investment."

I turned the pages of the contract and read the sections Claire pointed out. My brain felt like a machine with dusty gears. Normally I was the one using big words thanks to my English professor father, but contracts weren't written like novels. Authors wrote books in a way that readers could understand. Lawyers seemed to write on purpose to obscure the meaning.

I read the passages again. Claire did seem to have thought of everything.

The knots in my stomach that felt as hard as rocks still wouldn't ease.

Claire had a better mind for business than I did. It was part of why our partnership was proving to be such a good one, and part of why I'd let her talk me into a physical location in the first place. Up until a few months ago, when Claire first proposed it, owning a bakery had felt like a dream I'd never be able to reach. Up until that point, I'd been happy with my food truck. Claire had convinced me to at least let her try to make a physical bakery possible.

Maybe my hesitancy about parting with any more of my

business came from how hard I'd had to fight to keep my business going since I'd gone on the run from my husband. In a lot of ways, the business was the only thing that was truly mine. Isabel Addington wasn't even my real name. I lived in a rented room in a house that belonged to Claire.

All I had was my truck—once I replaced it—and my business.

Perhaps I didn't need the truck part of the equation anymore. The small food truck we'd priced out wouldn't be big enough for me to live in the way my original truck had been. And I'd made a promise to Dan not to run anymore. My heart had made a promise to Janie, even if I'd never spoken it out loud to her, not to leave her either. She'd already lost her biological parents. She didn't need to lose anyone else important to her until much later in life.

Claire tapped her foot. "Are you still reading?"

I set the contract down. It was making my eyes throb. "What if we didn't buy a new food truck? We could use that money to pay the additional rent."

Claire started shaking her head before I even finished. She pursed her lips into a line so thin that it reminded me of a caricature of an angry school teacher.

"We need a truck to run events. Our five-year plan still involves depending at least partly on things like the sandcastle competition and hot air balloon festival."

Claire flinched slightly over the last words. Our first year at the hot air balloon festival hadn't exactly been a success. A man had plunged to his death from a balloon, shutting down the event for days and sucking us into investigating his murder.

Claire did a little shiver-shake as if physically throwing off the memory. "Besides, running a truck at least seasonally is going to be one of our best forms of free advertisement. People see the truck around, at the beach, at events. Even if they don't buy from us right then, they might seek out the shop later."

So if we wanted to open a physical location, taking this deal was it. Our last chance. Months of searching had made it clear we weren't going to find another location in our price range. Everything else we'd toured was either in a poor location or would have needed more upgrades than we could afford.

This spot had been a bakery prior to the previous renter's retirement. We'd even spoken to the previous renter about buying at a discount the appliances he'd had put in. We'd certainly never find that anywhere else within our price range.

If we didn't take this chance, I'd have to let my dream of ever owning a bakery die and be buried.

I'd seen enough death in the past few years. I didn't need to watch my dream die too.

Claire reached for the folder where she'd filed all her calculations and projections. "Do you want to go over the numbers again?"

I shuddered. I'd rather be hung upside down by my ankles. "No. I'm in. Let's sign the papers."

*C*laire balanced the clipboard bearing the list of everything we needed to do before opening day on her knees. The list was long compared to the short amount of time we had before the date we'd selected for our opening day. We'd be working every day except Sundays to make it happen.

The new, smaller food truck bounced through a pothole. The clipboard on Claire's lap barely wobbled. She could have been a tightrope walker had life gone differently.

She poised a pen over the list. "Did you send the payment to Mr. Wendt?"

"Yesterday before the close of business."

Claire made a neat checkmark in the box she'd drawn next to that item on her list.

So far we'd basically checked off the big ticket items: buy the new-to-us food truck, purchase the commercial kitchen appliances from Mr. Wendt, the previous tenant, and sign the agreement with the building owner.

As soon as we picked up our keys—which would be within the next five minutes—we could start on all the smaller items on Claire's list.

I turned a corner, and the early morning sun burned into my eyes. I pulled the sunglasses my friend Eve had given me off the top of my head and slid them on.

Our new landlord has insisted we meet early, which was fine by me. We'd be starting our days early in order to bake everything fresh once we opened.

Claire squinted and leaned forward. "Looks like you might have to parallel park this thing on your first day driving it after all."

After climbing into the driver's seat of the new truck for the first time, I'd commented how I was glad I'd be able to get a parking spot before the street got crowded. I could parallel park a big truck. I just hated it. I always had nightmares of hitting one of the other cars and the cost of fixing the damage.

The street shouldn't be crowded at seven-thirty in the morning, though. Most of the businesses on this street didn't even open for another hour.

I looked where Claire was pointing. A bunch of vehicles did seem to be lining the road near our bakery. Shoot. I'd hoped to practice a few times before I had to parallel park for real. I'd been an expert at it with my old truck, but this one handled differently.

A cloud passed over the sun, and I lifted my sunglasses momentarily for a better look.

The cars up ahead weren't just parked on the sides of the road. They were parked all over, haphazardly. And there seemed to be people milling about in the street.

"Are those flashing lights?" Claire's voice sounded like she was being strangled.

They were. I could pick out the colors for both police vehicles and an ambulance.

Claire pressed both hands down on her clipboard. "That's not in front of our bakery."

If only speaking things could make them true.

The emergency vehicles were either in front of our bakery or one of the shops directly next door. Most likely they were there for one of the shops next door. They had to be. We weren't even open yet.

"An employee probably slipped or…" I couldn't think of anything else minor that would draw out both the police and paramedics. "I'll park down the street, so we're not in the way. We'll walk in."

Claire grasped her clipboard like it was a life preserver in a rough ocean. "We have plenty we can start on without needing the truck for today."

Even if we did need the truck, a small walk wouldn't hurt us.

Claire went to the gym more than most people went to their job, and I'd never minded a walk.

I parked the truck far enough back that it wouldn't impede the movement of the emergency vehicles.

We headed toward our bakery.

A few people clustered near the edge of the building. Yellow *Do Not Cross* crime scene tape blocked us from going any further.

The tape marked a neat box the size of our building. No matter how optimistic we wanted to be, there was no denying it. Whatever bad thing had happened to bring our emergency services had happened in our bakery,

"What's going on here?" Claire's voice was demanding. I almost expected her to slap the clipboard against her leg for emphasis.

"I heard what sounded like a gunshot when I got here to open." The young woman right next to me pointed at the cell phone store beside us, next to our bakery. "I called the police right away."

She looked to be in her mid-twenties. She wore a blue shirt and her hair pulled back in a bandana.

A police officer emerged from our bakery.

Claire waved her arm in the air. "Excuse me. This is our bakery. We need to get in there. What's going on?"

I cringed, and the young woman next to me stared at Claire with her mouth hanging open slightly. All I could think was that having Dan as her cousin had made her too relaxed with police officers. I wasn't quite as afraid of officers of the law as I had been before meeting Dan, but I still wouldn't have approached them with that level of entitlement.

The officer came over anyway. People always seemed to do what Claire told them to.

"You said this is your bakery?" the officer said.

Claire mentioned at me. "Our bakery, yes."

Normally I would have taken it as a compliment and a good sign for the future that Claire made sure people knew we were business partners. But this time I would have been perfectly content to have the police *not* notice me. I didn't know anything about what had happened here that could help them, and I didn't need them putting my name into the system. If I wasn't careful, it'd only be a matter of time before Jarrod figured out Isabel Addington and his wife Amy Miller were the same person.

And then he'd find me.

Paramedics emerged from our bakery building with a stretcher. A white sheet covered the face of the person on it.

The body on it. You didn't cover the face of a live person.

And only one person should have been in our bakery this morning—the owner.

I must have either let off a sound or lost all the color from my face because Claire cut off mid-sentence. Her gaze swiveled to where I was looking.

She gasped. "Is that Bob Jenner? We were supposed meet him here this morning. He owns the building."

"I'm sorry, ma'am. I can't divulge the identity of the victim until we've contacted next of kin."

He had to say that, but the chances that someone else had been in the bakery seemed slim. The young woman standing next to me said she called the police because she heard a gunshot. So someone shot Mr. Jenner. On the morning that we were supposed to pick up the key from him and take over our bakery.

If I believed in curses, I would have thought someone put one on me.

The officer Claire had flagged down ducked under the crime-scene tape. "I'll need both of you to come down to the station to answer a few questions to help us figure out what might have happened here."

Just when I thought this couldn't get worse, it did. I was in trouble.

The officer pulled out a pad of paper. "Give me your names and contact information, and I'll let the detective know you'll meet her at the station in a half hour."

My last hope of wriggling out of it vanished with the use of the female pronoun. Dan wasn't the detective assigned to this case. It was a female detective.

Claire rattled off our information before I could stop her. She gave my name as Isabel Addington.

The officer even took down our truck's license plate number.

My fingers felt numb. He'd only need to take that precaution if he thought there was a chance, however small, that we'd done this and might try to skip town. To him, we might have shot Mr. Jenner, run away when we heard the sirens, and then come back to make ourselves look innocent.

Claire pivoted on her heel. I trailed in her wake.

As soon as we were far enough away that I was sure no one would hear us, I came up beside her.

"You just lied to the police about my name. That's a crime."

Claire gave me an *I'm not stupid* look. "It's only a crime if *you* give the police a false name. I gave them the name I know you as. Whatever other names you might go by aren't any of my business."

I had no doubt Claire could sell that story, too, if anyone ever called her on it.

She picked up her pace. "Now call Dan and make sure he'll be there to run interference for you with the actual detective on this case. Because she's going to want you to state your name for the record, and we both know you can't do that."

3

*D*an met us inside the door of the police station twenty minutes later. "I spoke to Detective Austen. She understands the situation. For now, she's going to take notes from your interview by hand, and they won't be entered into the system."

All kinds of questions bubbled up inside. What exactly had he told her? What would happen once those notes did need to be logged? Or would they simply be shredded if what I had to say wasn't important to the case?

But I'd learned over the past few months that if there was one person in the world I could trust, it was Dan. His explanation had probably included that I'm a key witness in an upcoming murder trial, and that my real identity couldn't go in the system without putting my life in jeopardy right now. He may or may not have made it sound like the two things were connected rather than that I'd be in danger from my abusive husband, not the killer I was scheduled to testify against. Hopefully, if it were the latter, this would all be over before the investigating detective decided to ask more questions.

Dan squeezed my hand, quick and soft. Warmth shot through my body at the touch.

"It'll be okay," he whispered. "I promise."

Claire rolled her eyes. "Let's get this over with. We have too much work to do to spend all day here. Besides, I'm hoping they'll say this was all a mistake and that dead man isn't our brand-new landlord."

ALL DAY WAS ALMOST EXACTLY WHAT WE DID SPEND.

Detective Austen had dusky smears under her eyes, and her lips looked dry from all the interviews by the time she brought me back in the third time.

She didn't have the notepad with her this time. That could mean anything. I didn't know her well enough to guess.

I did know that bringing me back in a third time was all about trying to trip me up. They weren't convinced that Claire and I were telling the truth, even though I was sure we were saying the same thing. We'd been together and on our way to the bakery around the time the gunshots had been fired. At least, we had based on the time Detective Austen had asked me about twice now.

She leaned back in her chair and eyed me. Her look felt a bit like she was saying *what is it about you that justifies Dan Holmes sticking his neck out for you?*

I could have answered that for her if she'd asked it out loud—nothing. And yet, he kept doing it.

Not for the first time I wished Dan was the detective in charge of this case. He couldn't be because it was a conflict of interest given his relationship to Claire and me. If he had been, I wouldn't be here, bracing to answer questions I'd already answered twice before.

"We weren't able to confirm your alibi with the seller of your food truck. He can't remember the exact time you left."

Great. Last time she'd questioned me, she'd said that as soon as he confirmed when Claire and I finished with him, we'd be able to leave. Given the distance from there to our bakery, we wouldn't have been able to get there in time to shoot Mr. Jenner.

Now that the seller couldn't confirm our timeline, I apparently had to answer things again.

Her expression softened, but her eyes didn't. "I hope you can understand why that's a problem. We can't be sure where you and Ms. Cartwright were, and you can't give your real name."

I didn't react. She'd obviously been looking for a reaction

with that low blow. If Dan had told her why I couldn't have my real name in the system, she either wasn't sympathetic or she didn't believe I was telling the truth. Jarrod had told me for years that no one would believe me if I accused him of abuse—especially not other officers of the law. He'd convinced me to the point where it'd kept me from leaving for a lot longer than it should have. Even when I did leave, I hadn't gone to the police. I'd walked to the nearest church, and I'd avoided police officers up until Dan broke down my defenses.

I stayed perfectly still in my seat. "Detective Holmes has run a background check on my real name. He knows my reasons for wanting to withhold my real name are because I'm a victim, not because I've committed a crime."

She looked like she wanted to humph but was too self-controlled. "And you'd never met Robert Jenner? You signed a business deal with a man you'd never met?"

While I wasn't a naturally sarcastic person, she was pushing every button I had. Maybe she was a lovely person in real life, and this was her persona for interviewing persons of interest. That was possible. I was sure Dan wasn't the same Dan I knew in real life when he was in the interview rooms.

Still, I'd have a hard time putting this aside if I met her later under different circumstances.

I bit back a sigh. If I let the sigh out, she'd no doubt take it as snotty. "That's right. Claire is better at the business end than I am. She negotiated the contract, passed it by a lawyer, and then explained it to me. I trust her, so I signed."

Her eyebrows moved up together. She had to be intentionally baiting me, hoping she'd annoy me enough to lose my temper and admit to something.

If I'd been guilty of anything, she might have succeeded. I was so tired at this point, and the clock felt like it ticked louder with every minute I spent here. "I know you're just doing your job, and you want to do it well. I respect that because Mr. Jenner's death could hurt the career I've fought to keep for years. We had a good deal with him."

Her gaze on me felt hard and heavy. "Your contract says that if he dies within the first year, you get your share of the business back."

Of course she'd been able to get our contract. Nothing in our defense turned up during her search, but the one clause in the contract that gave us a motive, she found easily.

I took a deep breath. Claire had probably provided the contract for her, and she should have. It was the right move.

"If you have the contract, you also know that we're receiving a significant discount on the rental space. We couldn't afford to open a physical location without this deal. Now, whoever inherits this property might not want to make the same deal, and we might have to close."

My stomach ached at the mere thought. If we went forward

with the opening and that happened, we'd be in a hole we couldn't dig ourselves out of. We'd be out of business for good.

Detective Austen watched me for another ten seconds. She stood. "Thank you for spending your day here and for cooperating. We're done for now. You're free to head home."

Maybe it was my imagination, but I thought I heard her emphasize *for now*.

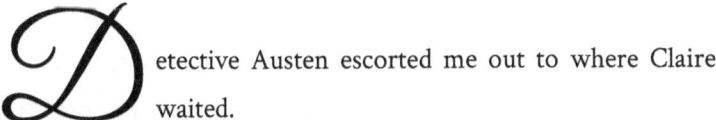

etective Austen escorted me out to where Claire waited.

Claire planted her hands on her hips and tilted her chin up. "Dan had to call Blake and ask him if Caroline could pick Janie up at school."

Blake was another one of the many Cartwright cousins. I'd met him when I was trying to prove I hadn't killed their grandfather, Harold. Initially, I'd tried to prove Blake had killed Harold for the inheritance until I found out there was no inheritance and Blake's suspicious behavior was him trying to find a job so he could take care of his wife and kids.

Janie would love going to their house to play until we could pick her up. But the tilt of Claire's chin said that wasn't the point. Everything about her said she'd expected better treatment from the police department because she was Dan's cousin, and I was his...friend.

"I'm sorry our murder investigation inconvenienced you," Detective Austen said.

I couldn't tell from her voice or expression whether she was being genuine or sarcastic.

Detective Austen turned on her heel. "I'll try to keep it quick next time I need to bring you in for questioning."

She tossed the words back over her shoulder, refusing Claire the chance for a rebuttal.

If Claire hadn't been so self-controlled, I would have expected her to stick out her tongue at Detective Austen's back. Maybe Detective Austen's growing annoyance and hostility toward me hadn't been about me at all. During our first interview, she'd seemed almost nice. But if Claire had been baiting her, it'd be no wonder if her mood went downhill.

"Were you that passive-aggressive in your interviews?"

Claire raised both eyebrows. "I'm an innocent person who wasn't even there at the time of the murder. She has no right to waste my entire day."

Technically, I think she did, but this wasn't a hill I wanted to die on with Claire. "We need to talk about what to do next. About the business."

Claire motioned for me to follow her. "My clipboard's in the truck. I can check it while you drive. We obviously can't get into the bakery now until the police release the scene and a cleaning crew comes in. Hopefully, I can adapt some things so we can get started. This has destroyed our timeline for opening day."

Normally, having to delay our opening by a few days wouldn't have been a big deal, but we'd called in favors. Alan Brooksbank had an article slated to run in The Positivity Project about how a near tragedy when I saved Janie after she'd been stung by a bee had resulted in a "sweet" business partnership. He'd even promised not to run any pictures of me, only of Claire. My friend Eve had volunteered her marketing expertise to help promote the opening day. The date was out there everywhere. If people showed up and we weren't open, it would cost us our momentum. Worse, they might never return.

But that hadn't been what I meant when I said we should talk about the business. "Can we still open at all now?"

"What are you talking about?" Claire yanked the food truck's passenger door and climbed in. "Of course we can."

She slammed the door as if that would be the end of the conversation.

I climbed in the driver's side.

Claire didn't look in my direction. "It'd be disastrous for the business if we pushed back the opening."

Confrontation wasn't my strength, but part of our agreement when we became business partners was that I would speak up. What I'd said to Detective Austen had been stuck in my mind ever since. "I'm not sure if we should go forward with the opening at all now."

Claire shot me the kind of look I would have expected had I suggested we roast Janie's cat Pirate for supper.

I left the truck in park. I wasn't sure I could get this all out coherently if I had to focus on traffic as well. "If we keep going forward with our plans and then we can't open on time, we increase our chances of the business failing in the first year. And that's not taking into account what happens if the new landlord refuses to cut us the same deal on the rent."

I didn't need to spell out for Claire the way I had for Detective Austen that we couldn't afford the full rent. That if we put everything we had into setting up the bakery and then couldn't pay the rent, we'd lose it all. Claire knew it as well as I did. It was why she'd brokered the odd agreement in the first place.

"We don't have the space in this truck to make a full-time go of it, especially not once winter sets in." Claire's tone was matter of fact.

She was right. We also couldn't afford a bigger truck unless the previous owner of this one would take back the vehicle less than twenty-four hours after we bought it *and* if Mr. Wendt would return our money for the appliances. Unless we could get all that money back, and our first and last month's rent from Mr. Jenner's estate, we wouldn't be able to buy a bigger food truck.

And then we'd be giving up on what had become a shared dream.

I could almost see Claire doing the same mental math I'd done. "Call the man and see if we can return this truck. If we can't, it's a moot point, and we have to go forward with the opening."

I nodded and dialed. "This is How Sweet It Is, the cupcake ladies."

He made a noise like he was only half listening.

"We were wondering if we could return the truck for a full refund."

"Is there something wrong with it?"

I could lie to him, and he'd take the truck back for sure. Well, maybe not for sure. He might offer to have it repaired on his dime. Since there wasn't anything actually wrong, that wouldn't work.

Besides, lying about the truck felt wrong. I didn't think God would look kindly on us lying for our own benefit, at the potential expense of someone else.

"There's nothing wrong. We've just decided we want to go a different route."

"No can do. Check your bill of sale. I wrote right on there that the sale was final."

Claire must have heard because she was already fishing around in the glove compartment for it. Her gaze skimmed over it, and she shoved it back in with enough force to tell me it said exactly that.

We hadn't paid any attention at the time to language like that because returning the truck hadn't crossed either of our minds.

"We've run into some problems with opening our business,

and we need the money from this truck. Isn't there anything you can do?"

"I could give you half back. I'll need to keep the rest as a storage fee. Who knows how long it'll have to sit around before I can resell it."

Claire reached for my phone as if she were going to give him a tongue-lashing. I kept it away from her.

"Half isn't enough," I said. "We need a full refund."

"You want the full amount back, you'll have to resell the truck yourself to someone else."

He hung up on me.

"We just have to make it work," Claire said, as if it would be easy as long as we put our minds to it. "We're strong. We've overcome bigger obstacles."

"We have overcome worse." I wasn't a natural optimist, but I forced myself to repeat the words. Words had power. "We'll make it work."

5

Claire burst into the house. The front door slammed against the wall in a way that she would have yelled at Janie for. "They released the scene. I already picked up the key from the police station."

I set aside the gum paste vegetables I'd been creating. One of our regular clients, philanthropist Elijah Wells, was meeting with the city councilors to get their approval to re-zone an area of Lakeshore. He wanted to build an allotment where people who didn't have any space for vegetable gardens could grow some of their own food. He'd decided that meant he needed to woo them not only with cupcakes that included vegetables like carrot, zucchini, and beet, but also that the top of each cupcake needed to look like a little vegetable patch. I'd been forming teeny tiny carrots, cabbages, watermelons, and eggplants all morning.

At this point, I could barely see straight. "What about the trauma cleaners?"

"I just got off the phone with them. They finished up late last night."

That was a good sign. It meant that the gunshot hadn't created a lot of blood spatter. Either that, or the cleaners were exceptionally fast. Claire had said the space was basically empty except for the display cases and appliances, so that could have contributed as well.

We might be able to make our opening day after all.

"Let me grab my stuff."

Claire turned on her heel. "I'll be waiting in the car."

CLAIRE AND I STOOD SIDE BY SIDE, STARING AT THE LARGE FRONT windows of the shop. Or, more specifically, at the red spray-painted words graffitied across them. They had to have been scrawled there sometime between last night and this morning since the trauma cleaners hadn't cleaned them off or mentioned them.

Claire tilted her head to the side. "I think the first two words are *keep out* and the last one is *slut*."

I wasn't sure what was more surreal—hearing Claire say the word *slut* or staring at it written on our windows when we were already one headache away from missing our opening day.

I mirrored her tilted head. Because what else was there to do. The words were smeared enough that I couldn't be sure whether Claire was right or wrong. I couldn't make out the third of the four words at all. Given the tone of the message it was probably a curse word.

A crazy laugh bubbled up inside me. It was laugh or cry. "Maybe it's just a gang tag and not words at all."

Claire tilted her head in the other direction. "You might be right." She sighed. "You want to flip a coin to see who gets to search the internet for what takes spray paint off glass and who has to tell Detective Austen that her crime scene was vandalized."

That made it sound like the scene was contaminated before the police cleared it. Still, it seemed like too much of a coincidence that someone spray painted over the front window shortly after a murder happened here. Detective Austen did need to know.

And Claire's tone made it clear that she didn't want to ever deal with Detective Austen again. Given how she and Detective Austen would probably rather both chew on old rubber than speak to each other again, it was probably better I made the call anyway.

"You do the search," I said, "I'll call the detective. This time."

"There better not be a next time," Claire said.

I pulled out my phone, called the police station, and asked for Detective Austen.

The man at the front desk put me through.

"Austen," she answered.

"I'm one of the women from How Sweet It Is Bakery. You interviewed me about the Bob Jenner murder case. He was our landlord."

I paused to make sure she had time to figure out who I was since I hadn't given my name.

"Yes?" she said. There was a hint of excitement in her voice, as if she was hoping I actually did know something about the murder that would make her job easier.

Just the opposite, in fact.

"When we arrived at the building this morning, we found that someone had spray painted our window."

A pause. The line filled with the white noise of other people in the background. "You called to tell me that your business was vandalized? That's not my area. I investigate murders."

I was trying hard not to judge her and not to dislike her. This could be her professional persona. She might be a lovely person in real life and with her coworkers. For Dan's sake, I hoped so. I hated to think of him having to regularly work with such an unpleasant person.

Or Claire might have gotten under her skin like a splinter that refused to come out, and I was guilty by association. Claire did sometimes have that effect on people.

"It just seemed unlikely to us that a crime would occur at the same place twice so closely together unless they were related."

Detective Austen made an *mmm* sound. "This is the mistake that people who like to watch too many crime shows make. Unlikely doesn't mean impossible. This was very likely a random vandalism."

Part of me wanted to tell her that I didn't watch crime shows. I hadn't even had access to a TV for years until I moved in with Claire. But trying to defend myself wouldn't get me results. "Have other businesses in the area been vandalized?"

"I wouldn't know." Detective Austen spoke slowly as if I would have trouble understanding if she spoke at a normal pace. "I don't investigate vandalism. I'd recommend you call the front desk and have them direct you to the proper department."

She hung up on me. What was it with people hanging up on me lately? Didn't they care that it was rude?

I shifted to face Claire.

"That looked like it went well," she said. "I did find a way to get the paint off, so at least we're not zero for two. And since you handled the wicked witch detective, I'll call and report the vandalism to someone else. We can't start to clean this up until we've reported it and had it photographed."

I gave her a grateful smile. Somehow talking with Detective Austen had given me a headache.

Worse, my gut told me Detective Austen was wrong. While it wasn't impossible that the vandalism and murder weren't connected, the odds seemed to be in favor of some sort of link. I squinted at the words again. Figuring out the connection would be a lot easier if the person who spray painted the windows had taken a little more time to make his or her message clear.

I snapped a quick photo with my phone so I could look at it again later.

Behind me, I could hear Claire reporting the vandalism to another officer. Even if they thought it was worth giving their time to—which wasn't likely to happen since catching a vandal was almost impossible if they weren't stopped in the act—they wouldn't have anywhere to start looking for the vandal if Detective Austen refused to acknowledge a connection.

I glanced at Claire. Whoever had done this was actively hindering my dream. It'd taken me a long time to be brave enough to dream and hope for anything again. Letting some faceless bully stop me now felt wrong and weak. I'd be letting this person take from me what I'd fought for despite the threat Jarrod posed.

And it wasn't only my dream at stake. It was Claire's dream too. She'd put so much into this. After all the time we'd spent together, she was really starting to feel like the bossy older sister I'd never had. I couldn't let her down.

Quitting now, or waiting and hoping this person didn't strike again, meant giving up both our dreams. We wouldn't get another chance at this.

If Detective Austen refused to look for a connection, then she left me no choice. I would.

6

_T_he officer who arrived over an hour later squinted at the spray painted writing. He shrugged. "You got me for what it says. It's not a gang tag, I can tell you that much. Someone tried to write something specific, but it looks like they didn't know what they were doing."

Claire and I had surmised that much ourselves already.

The officer stepped back and aimed the digital camera he'd brought at the front of our store.

Claire hovered next to him. "You're going to collect fingerprints as well, aren't you?"

"Yes, ma'am, I will." He snapped another shot from a different angle. "But I have to tell you, unless the prints are already in the system, we're not likely to catch the person who did this. A vandal who gets away usually gets off free."

That wasn't exactly encouraging, but we'd guessed that much

as well while we were waiting. It was like when someone smashed a car window, grabbed something lying inside, and ran. The police department didn't have the resources to follow up on petty crimes, and with no witnesses, they didn't even have a place to start.

The officer collected fingerprints and even a hand print off the windows.

Claire let out a sigh long enough that it seemed like it should have taken more air than she could have held in her body. "Most of those prints probably belong to the police."

"Probably."

The officer packed up his kit and took Claire's statement. She made sure only her name went on the police report. It wasn't like I was actually a witness to anything. My inclusion wasn't necessary, and it spared us the fake-name problem.

He finished writing and ripped a sheet off his clipboard. "You can give this copy to your insurance company for your claim."

He climbed back into his cruiser.

Claire glared at the paper in her hand as if it'd been the one to offend her. "There's no money in the budget to pay the deductible on a claim."

We technically had a buffer built into our plans. The problem was that if we spent it on getting the paint professionally cleaned off, we wouldn't have what we needed if we encountered a problem with the opening that we couldn't handle ourselves. "How long would it take for them to send someone to take care of this?"

Claire folded the police report into a precise square and slid it into her pocket. "There's no time in the budget to wait for them either."

Filing an insurance claim meant waiting for them to process the claim and then waiting for a spot in the schedule of whatever professional cleaner they contracted with. If that took anywhere near as long as receiving the check for my destroyed food truck had, we'd be opening with questionable words emblazoned across our windows for sure. "I guess we're putting in sweat equity then."

"I think there's a ladder in the back," Claire said. "We'd better get started. I have a whole list that we need to complete if we want any hope of opening on schedule."

AN HOUR LATER, OPENING WITH THE GRAFFITI STILL ON THE windows was sounding like a better idea every second. We'd only finished the first word, and my arms felt like they were no longer attached to my body.

Below me, Claire paused and kneaded her lower back. "I clearly need to add more squats, bending, and kneeling exercises into my routine."

That might have prepared her for this, but probably not.

Claire was fit from her daily workouts, but she was also twenty years older than me. We just weren't created to abuse our bodies as much the older we got.

My legs trembled slightly from bracing myself on the ladder without using my hands. I climbed down. "Do you want to trade for a bit?"

Claire glanced at the ladder and shuddered. "No, thank you."

I wiped my forehead on my sleeve. Normally I'd have loved such a beautiful fall day, but today the sunshine just added one more layer of discomfort to what we needed to do. "What was supposed to be on the list for today?"

Claire shook her head. "You don't want to know."

Which was as good as saying that this might be the straw that broke the camel's back or the nail in the coffin or the multitude of other clichés that said we could only endure so much before our plans couldn't recover in time for the opening.

"Excuse me?" a young male voice said from the other side of where Claire stood.

I jumped, and Claire straightened out of her slumping posture. We both turned.

How tired and worried about the bakery was I that I hadn't even heard someone approach? That wasn't like me. Or maybe it was becoming the new me. I seemed to be sleeping a little more soundly at night as well, if how rested I now felt in the morning was any indication.

Still, it'd been a good thing I hadn't been up on the ladder when he spoke or I might have spent the rest of the day in the ER from a fall. Then we really wouldn't have been able to open on time.

The young man took another step toward us. He looked like he was in his late teens, with strategically mussed brown hair. His form was tall and lanky in that way that some young men had when they were still growing in spurts. His cheeks weren't entirely smooth, but he didn't look like he'd be able to grow a beard worthy of Duck Dynasty either.

He pointed at the three words of graffiti we still had left. "I could finish that for you."

Claire planted her hands on her hips, a sure sign that she was mentally assessing our budget.

"I wouldn't ask for much." His words tumbled out over each other as if he could see Claire preparing to send him on his way as well. "Consider it a trial run. And if you're happy with my work, maybe you'd consider hiring me on even part-time once you open." He looked away as if he was too embarrassed to meet our eyes for the next part. "I really need the work. I'm trying to save for college."

My heart felt like it cracked a little. I knew what that felt like, to want something and not have the money to achieve it. To not know if it would ever be possible. Claire should understand that too.

I held up a *wait here* finger at the young man and pulled Claire far enough away that we could discuss it.

"Surely we can find something in the budget to hire him to finish this."

Claire glared at the rag and bucket of water she'd been using in a way that made me think she wanted to kick them over. "We'd have to use some of our emergency-fund money."

"If graffiti doesn't count as an emergency, I don't know what does. We need to be spending time on what was actually on the list for today."

Claire looked over at where the boy still stood. Spend money we didn't have or be almost guaranteed to miss our opening day —the war was written all across her face.

She turned back to face him. "How much would you want?"

7

*C*laire added more paint to her roller. Apparently, moving from cleaning off the graffiti to what needed to be done within the store was like the proverbial out of the frying pan and into the fire. But at least I wasn't on a ladder out in the hot sun.

And the fresh paint was already making a huge difference in how bright and clean the space looked.

Claire swiped the roller over the wall with a precision that only she could bring to painting. "I'm surprised the new owner hasn't contacted us about rent. I'm going to call them today and see if I can convince them to take the same deal. I doubt it, but I need to try."

"I wouldn't bother," the young man's voice said from close behind me.

I dropped my paint brush. It landed with a splat on the old

sheets we'd laid down, barely missing my socks.

We'd left the door open to air out the paint fumes, but that kid must have ninja training. His movements were unnaturally quiet.

I picked up my paint brush and turned around.

He set the bucket and scrub brush near the display counter. "If it was me, I wouldn't. Worst case, you have to pay a couple months' back rent once the new owner figures out you haven't been paying anything. Best case, you get a couple months' free rent."

He shrugged like the logic was obvious.

To most people, it might have been. But Claire and I were Christians, which meant we were supposed to live in a way that would please God. Neither of us were perfect, but I, for one, didn't want to be one of those people who claimed to be a Christian and then lived like everyone else in the world. Too many people who called themselves Christians turned others away from God by their bad behavior.

I laid my brush across the top of the paint can. "I wouldn't feel right doing something like that. We wouldn't be any better than squatters then."

"Besides," Claire bent down and tried to move some spilled paint from the sheet back into her paint pan—we had just enough to do what we needed to, "a stunt like that would probably cost us the chance of convincing the new owner to make the same deal."

The young man crossed the distance between them and held the pan for her. "You got some kind of special deal from the last owner?"

"We did. We—" Claire froze, her gaze fixed on a spot on the far wall. "Please tell me that clock is wrong."

Both the young man and I swiveled to face the clock. I pulled out my cell phone. The time matched.

"It's accurate."

"Crap." Claire straightened up so fast she almost tipped the whole paint tray over. "I still need to make a supply run for the appetizers for this weekend's wedding. If I don't get there today, it'll be almost impossible for me to have everything prepared and do what we need to here."

We'd been hired to cater a small wedding where the bride and groom were only doing appetizers and a cupcake tree rather than a sit-down dinner. I'd been making edible flowers every day leading up to today because I planned to bake the cupcakes fresh the day of the wedding and add the decorations right before delivery.

Claire wouldn't make it to the store in time to buy what she still needed if she also had to make calls to figure out who our new landlord was.

Helping Claire with the phone call so that she could buy what she needed gave me a good excuse to contact the landlord's next of kin. That seemed like as reasonable a place as any to start figuring out who had enough of a grudge against him or their family to keep vandalizing the store even after he was gone. Since the vandalism happened after his murder, hopefully his family would want to help and be willing to talk to me about it. Now that the criminal had acted twice, it gave us twice the evidence, even if Detective Austen didn't think so.

I took the paint roller from Claire's hand. "Go. I'll clean this up and then call our former landlord's business number. Hopefully someone will answer and be able to give us the name and number of whoever our new landlord is."

Claire looked down at her paint spattered clothes and made an *oh well* gesture with her hands. She grabbed her purse and speed walked out the door. If I was lucky, she'd remember to come back for me afterward since we'd driven her car here. Claire could sometimes be a little hyper-focused.

The young man flopped a wave at me and headed toward the door as well. The windows he'd washed were so clear I wouldn't have guessed they ever had paint on them.

"Wait. Don't you want your pay?"

He looked back over his shoulder. "I'll be back tomorrow to see if there's any more work you need me to do." He glanced around the room that it'd taken us as long to paint as it had for him to clean off the seemingly permanent spray paint. "If you have another room that needs painting, for example."

We did still need to paint the restroom and the kitchen, if we had enough paint left.

He was out the door before I could even ask his name. It was a good tactic. If we'd paid him, that would conclude our agreement, and we might decide not to give him any more work. If he waited to get paid, he risked us not paying him, but he also had a reason to come back. He could find us in a position like today where we had too much to do and not enough time or energy to do it. He was a smart kid, I'd give him that, even if he was a little odd.

And I must be getting old if I was thinking about a teenager as a kid.

I finished the two-foot section of wall that was left and then cleaned everything up. We couldn't waste anything, so that had to be done before I made my phone call. If the call took a while and the paint hardened, I'd have to face the wrath of Claire. Not even Dan with his years on the police force and working undercover wanted to do that.

With everything put away, I dialed the phone number we had for our former landlord.

"Jenner Developments," a voice that sounded like it belonged to a middle-aged woman said. She also sounded congested, as if she'd been crying.

I needed to choose my words carefully. The poor woman was probably grieving her boss if he was a good one and potentially worrying about her job. This was the part I always struggled with when someone who seemed like a good person died. What had he done to end up murdered?

"I'm from How Sweet It Is, and we recently signed a rental

agreement with Mr. Jenner. I need to get in touch with whoever will be taking over his business."

"Oh, yes, umm..." The sounds of her clicking on her keyboard filled the space. "Let me get you the phone number for Mr. Jenner's lawyer. He's handling his estate, so he'd be the one you'd need to speak to."

From what Claire had told me, Jenner Developments was a small business staff-wise. Mr. Jenner preferred to handle a lot of the business himself, but even he would need a lawyer for legal matters.

"Thank you. And I'm sorry for your loss."

I wrote down the lawyer's phone number. I called the number, introduced myself once I was connected to the lawyer himself, and explained that we needed the name and phone number of who our new landlord would be.

"All his property will be going to a family member, but they haven't decided yet what to do about the property." The lawyer's voice was nasally, and his tone sounded annoyed that he would have to deal with someone like me. "They might sell it."

That was even worse than we'd expected. If the building was sold, the new owner might not want to rent it out at all. They certainly wouldn't be willing to give us the same deal as Claire had negotiated with Bob Jenner. Our only hope of getting the same deal was that whoever inherited would want to respect Mr. Jenner's final wishes.

"You'll be contacted once the estate is settled with the family's decision," the lawyer said.

We needed a chance to talk to the person who would inherit before they made any decisions. That way, we could at least plead our case.

But the lawyer had been careful to not reveal so much as the gender of the family member set to inherit.

I hadn't mentioned the vandalism because we'd taken care of it ourselves without even going through our rental insurance. Perhaps that would give me a way in.

"We'd appreciate knowing what the new owner plans to do. I'd still really like to speak to them in the meantime. We were vandalized last night, and we were hoping to speak to the owner about security."

"Already taken care of." His tone was definitely brusque, as if he were hoping this would finally wrap up the conversation. "A security company will be coming out to install security cameras within the next couple of days. Now, if that's all, I have clients I need to attend to."

Of course, they would already know about it. The police probably called Mr. Jenner's lawyer as soon as we filed the report since he was handling the estate.

I was out of ideas at the moment for anything that might convince him to give me so much as a hint about who the new owner might be. "That's all."

---

8

*C*laire and I stared at the clock on the wall. I couldn't speak for her, but I felt like we were back staring at the spray paint on our windows a few days ago.

"We gave it our best," I said.

"We failed you mean."

The words hit me hard enough to make my chest hurt.

You wouldn't be able to survive without me, Jarrod used to say. *Weak. Failure. Worthless.*

This had been my chance to prove him wrong. More than that, it was the dream I thought I'd never get a chance to have thanks to the bad choice I'd made in my marriage partner.

And I'd let myself think that this time, finally, what I wanted out of life was going to work out despite the setbacks.

"Maybe we can still do it. What does your checklist say for how much time we'd need?"

Claire picked it up from the top of the display counter. The list would tell us if there was any hope at all. Claire had not only written down everything we needed to do. She'd put it in the most efficient order, assigned a time block to it for how long it should take, and came up with a tentative schedule. The last one had been obliterated the day Bob Jenner died. Even with our teenage helper—whose name turned out to be Scott—working with us all day today, we hadn't been able to catch up. He'd apologized multiple times about needing to leave when he did, and once again, he'd said he'd be back tomorrow, and we could pay him then.

Claire's lips moved silently, a sign she was mentally adding totals. "Two days' worth at best. Maybe as much as three."

It was already after five at night, and we were supposed to open tomorrow morning. Even working through the night, we wouldn't be able to complete two to three days' work.

Claire tossed the clipboard back onto the counter. It landed with a clatter. "I'll text Dan and tell him he won't need to bring us supper. We might as well go home since there's no chance we'll be ready for the opening even with an all-nighter."

Claire's words mirrored my own thoughts so closely that it felt like pouring alcohol into the wound.

I'd been working on my relationship with God, praying, reading the Bible, and attending church with Dan, Janie, and Claire. But at times like this it felt like God didn't care about someone like me. Someone who had screwed up her life so badly and had ignored and blamed him for so long. It felt like he was letting me have the consequences of my life choices to make sure I'd learn my lesson.

That wasn't the God that the pastor preached about or Dan talked about, but that's how it felt. How did I even know God was there and listening?

I sighed and headed back to the kitchen, leaving Claire texting in the front room. There was still work to do. The chances of the business failing because we missed our opening day—with all the press and buzz we'd planned—were higher, but who knew. It'd take a miracle to succeed now, but it wasn't completely impossible.

Believing in miracles is a crutch for the weak-minded, Jarrod used to say.

Sometimes I was afraid he was right. He'd always mocked religion, repeating back to me all the things that were popularly shared in the news and society. As a person who'd grown up in a Christian home, I saw the holes in his logic and the caricatures he painted, but I'd never been brave enough to speak up. Instead, I'd been angry enough at God and already scared enough of my husband that I pretended to agree with him.

Maybe things would have been different if I'd had faith to hang on to and I could have believed what the Bible said about me more than what Jarrod said about me. Maybe I'd have had the self-confidence to leave him sooner.

Without a time machine, I'd never know what might have been.

A knock sounded on the front door. Probably someone thinking we were already open. Claire was out front, so she could handle it.

I wasn't sure I could.

Claire gasped.

Icy tingles flashed over my skin. Had the person who murdered Mr. Jenner come back?

I lunged for the door separating the kitchen from the rest of the shop. If someone had forced their way in, I needed to call 9-1-1 before they knew I was here.

I peeked out.

Dan, Blake, and three women who looked like family too, based on their features, stood in the shop. Claire had one of them in a hug that was tight enough I was surprised she hadn't squeezed the woman's eyeballs out. What was going on?

I exited the kitchen.

"Isabel!" Claire practically shrieked my name. She waved at me. "Come here."

Her cheeks were damp as if she'd been crying. I'd never seen Claire cry. Not even at her grandfather's funeral.

"You know Blake already."

He grinned at me.

Claire pointed at each of the women. "This is Stacey."

That was a name I recognized. When I first met Blake, and

we were talking about the grandchildren helping with their grandfather's living expenses, he'd said Stacey had helped until her mom needed an expensive operation.

"How's your mom?" I asked.

She drew her chin back, and her eyes widened slightly as if she couldn't believe I would remember a detail like that about someone I'd never met. "She's doing really well, but she hates sticking to her new diet and going to physio."

Claire pointed to the next two women in line. The younger one had a nose ring and hair that looked too black to be her natural color. The older woman beside her shared her cheekbones and blue eyes. The resemblance between them was even closer than between all the others, probably a mother and daughter.

"And this," Claire said, "is Haley and Wendy."

I smiled at each of them in turn even though I didn't feel like it. If they'd come to get a look at the place before opening, their timing was all wrong. Surely Dan would have realized that after Claire's text.

"What are you all doing here?" I addressed the question to Dan.

The smile he gave me made me feel warm down into the tips of my toes. "We couldn't let you miss your opening day."

"What good is having a big family," Blake said, "if we can't at least show up when you need us most."

That almost sounded like he was including me, but I wasn't

family. He must have meant Claire was their family. As her business partner, I'd benefit as well.

Stacey waved a hand at the room. "I've got my toolbox in the truck, so Danny and I can work on setting up tables, building any remaining shelving, hanging pictures, whatever you need."

I smirked at Dan. I hadn't ever heard him called Danny before. Stacey looked about our age, so my guess was she'd been one of the cousins that he played with as a child.

He and Stacey exited the shop, presumably to collect the tools she'd mentioned.

Blake craned his neck to look past me. "She's a master carpenter, so she's the one to trust with that." He edged past me, moving me out of the way by the shoulders so fast that my body didn't even have time to panic at the contact. "You'd be better off putting me in the kitchen. I have experience now, and seniors can be picky customers."

That was right. Dan had mentioned that Blake recently got a job working in the kitchen of a senior's residence. It had to feel good after he'd been unemployed for so long.

My heart felt like my chest cavity was too small to hold it. These people weren't my family, and I'd only met most of them today. So why did they feel so much like family?

The teenager with the nose ring forged after him. Haley, Claire had introduced her as. "I can measure stuff too, Blake. It's not *that* hard."

Wendy laid a hand on my shoulder. "Like we told Claire,

we're your hands wherever you need us, for as long as you need us, to make sure this place opens tomorrow like it's supposed to."

I understood why Claire had been crying. My own eyes felt tight and hot. "Thank you."

Wendy gave two hearty pats on my shoulder. "It's not all altruistic. We couldn't pass up the chance to meet the woman who got Claire out of her funk over that piece-of-dirt husband of hers."

"Or the one who got Uncle Dan dating again," Haley called from the kitchen.

Heat flared up my cheeks. If Haley meant me, that Dan and I were dating, there'd been a huge misunderstanding.

I swiveled to face Claire. She knew I couldn't date. Surely she'd help me by clearing that up. Besides, how did the extended family even know about me other than as Claire's business partner? Did Dan talk about me?

Claire gave me a *let it be* shoulder shrug. If I hadn't known better, I would have thought she was holding back a smile.

Dan and Stacey set to work out front with Claire directing them. Blake, Haley, Wendy, and I clustered in the kitchen. I set each of them tasks.

For one heartbeat, I watched them work. Maybe God still heard my prayers after all.

*H*aley turned on the oven for our first batch of cupcakes. Or, more accurately, she tried to turn it on. Nothing happened.

Blake nudged her with his elbow. "I know you break technology by looking at it, but I didn't know that extended to appliances or I'd have turned the oven on myself."

Haley stuck her tongue out at him. "I didn't break it!"

My cheeks felt tired from smiling. Even when my dad was alive, it'd been just the two of us. I'd never been in the middle of a larger family with a good, close relationship. I hadn't realized what I was missing.

What was going on finally filtered through. I set aside the buttercream roses I'd been piping onto small slips of parchment. "Let me try it."

Haley moved aside to give me space.

I pressed the buttons, but I got the same warning code that Haley had. It'd worked before. I tested all the appliances and other equipment before I paid the former renter for. My limbs felt heavy. We couldn't survive one more set back. If the oven was broken, we'd really be done. Not even the whole Cartwright family showing up would save us.

"I'll call the man who sold them to us and see if he's ever had a similar problem." I pulled out my phone and dialed his number. A man's voice answered on the third ring. "Is this Mr. Wendt?"

"It is."

"This is Isabel from How Sweet It Is. We bought your bakery equipment, and the stove stopped working. I was wondering if you had any ideas about it."

There was a squeaking-creaking noise in the background that sounded like him settling into a recliner chair. "It was the stove that stopped working you say."

"Dad," a man's voice said on his end, faint but not so soft as to be hard to hear, "do you want me to go check on the oven?"

"Naw, naw," Mr. Wendt said. "It's an easy fix. It happened all the time. Has anyone moved or bumped the oven since you used it last?"

Considering the last time I turned it on was before Bob Jenner died, that was a certainty. The trauma cleaners would have moved it when they were cleaning. "Yes."

"There's a shut-off valve for the gas that's too sensitive. Every time my Annie cleaned, we had to turn the valve back on."

Blake must have heard because he leaned around the oven. "Got it."

Haley rushed forward and pressed the buttons. The poof of the oven firing up sounded clearly.

"You saved us before we're even open." I hoped he could hear the smile and the relief in my voice. "I'll owe you a dozen cupcakes in thanks. What's your address? I'll even personally deliver them."

He gave me his address. "But a visit would be enough of a thanks. I don't get out much anymore, and seeing a pretty young lady would brighten my day."

I wasn't really either of those things. I couldn't begin to imagine what he looked like, but my mental picture was building of a bald man with a mustache and suspenders. "How do you know I'm young? Or pretty? I don't want to disappoint you."

"I'm a seventy-year-old man with age spots and a bum hip. If you're under fifty-five and can walk without a cane, you'll be young and pretty to me."

I laughed out loud. I'd never tell Claire that she wouldn't be considered young by Mr. Wendt.

I ended the call and started on the lemon curd we'd need once the first batch of cupcakes came out of the oven. Haley already had the muffin tins almost filled with batter.

I'd set a time to visit Mr. Wendt next week, but suddenly I wished it was earlier. I'd assumed he closed his business because of age. And maybe he had. He had said he was over seventy and had a bum hip.

With everything that happened here so far, though, maybe he'd closed his shop for other reasons. Claire had been so focused on finding us a location we could afford, on a street with enough traffic to make financial sense, that she hadn't thought to look up crime statistics for this neighborhood. I hadn't thought about it either. The street *looked* safe. Neither of us had enough experience with real estate to have considered looks could be deceiving.

Claire and I were willing to fight through the challenges of crimes taking place in and around our place of business because we had energy, and we were young. If we didn't work How Sweet It Is, we'd both need to find other work to support ourselves.

If bad things started happening, and I was retirement age anyway, I might not have fought so fiercely. I might have decided I'd had a good run of it and should leave before anything worse happened.

Talking to Mr. Wendt would give me the perfect opportunity to find out if this neighborhood was a crime hot spot or if we were being targeted for some reason.

10

"Scott's coming in again today, isn't he?" I asked Claire as I unlocked the bakery for our second week.

The street around us was so quiet this early in the morning that I could hear the electric hum of the street lamps. My voice sounded like a shout with the way it seemed to echo off the buildings. I'd seen Lakeshore at this time of day before, but never in this way. Before I'd been awake out of fear while the city slept.

Claire yawned so largely that her jaw popped. "We'll need to make his position official soon. Once he hits full-time hours, we have to make all the government contributions."

Only Claire would be able to manage something like that while half awake. But she was right.

Our first week had been so busy that we'd ended up needing Scott's help every day so that I could spend most of my time in the kitchen. "If it stays this busy."

Claire gave me a look that said *don't jinx it.* "We'll need him to fill out the paperwork regardless today. If we let it go on any longer, we could be accused of paying him under the table."

The muscles in my neck tensed at the thought of an IRS agent poking into our business and asking questions. Questions that would require a name and SSN from me.

"I'll get everything set out, and he can do it today."

If it stayed this busy, we'd likely need to hire someone else as well as Scott. Once he saved up enough to start college and had classes to attend, he wouldn't be able to work as many hours.

Claire headed straight for the kitchen, but I turned off into our office.

I froze halfway to the desk. Something was off. The hair on my arms stood up as if I'd been hit by a gust of icy wind.

The room was small enough that I knew there wasn't someone hiding in it. I looked behind that door to be sure anyway.

Whatever it was, wasn't as obvious as that.

I'd shushed Fear so many times in the past months that his voice in my head was an indistinct moan rather than words.

I ran my gaze over the desk again. The top lay clear except for a pen, a notebook Claire and I jointly used to jot things down if we were too busy to follow up on them immediately, and a stack of papers.

On the right side of the desk.

I'd stacked them on the left. I was sure of it. They'd been on the right side, but I'd gone to write a note before we left last night, and I bumped them. I moved them to the left where they were less likely to end up strewn across the floor.

I inched around the desk. One of the drawers stood a half inch ajar.

Someone had been in here. They'd been careful when they finished looking through things. Careful enough that most people might not have noticed.

I wasn't most people. I had to notice everything, track everything, because when Jarrod found me, the signs wouldn't be big. They'd be small. Like this. Something bumped that he hadn't noticed or placed back slightly off kilter.

In my food truck, I had a routine. I placed everything in a specific place, in a specific way. No one could have rifled through my belongings there without me noticing.

I grabbed a pen, stuck it in the drawer handle, and pulled open the drawer. Everything inside looked the way I'd left it.

I glanced at the door. Claire would be expecting me back in the kitchen any minute. I couldn't let her know about this. The last time she'd been loosely connected to an investigation, she hadn't been able to sleep. With our landlord already murdered in this building, and the vandalism before we even opened, one more thing could send her careening back down that unhealthy path.

But I couldn't let it pass either. Not after everything else that had gone on.

I edged the door closed so that Claire would be less likely to overhear and dialed Dan's number. Even though it was pre-dawn early, he'd be up. He'd be headed to work for an early shift. I knew because we hadn't been able to take Janie for him, and she'd spent last night having a sleepover with Blake's kids.

"Is everything alright?" Dan asked instead of a hello.

"I'm not sure." I kept my voice low and explained to him about the papers and the drawer.

"Could Claire have moved things?" he asked when I finished.

That was possible. But I remembered being the last one in the office before we closed up and went home. Still, I couldn't be sure of that without asking Claire. And if I asked Claire, I put her mental wellbeing at risk. Last time, she'd stopped sleeping and had been up in the night cleaning. She'd gone to the gym multiple times a day. Nothing seemed to help until I finally convinced her to see a therapist.

She was still going months later.

"I'm not trying to downplay your concerns." Dan was one of the few people I believed when he said something like that. He'd earned the right to tell me when I was potentially over-reacting because he'd always taken me seriously in the past. "Whoever murdered Bob Jenner and vandalized the store wouldn't have a reason to riffle through your files and then try to put them back in a way you wouldn't notice. Everything they've done so far hasn't been subtle. And your files aren't anything that would interest them."

I leaned against the door. The sounds of Claire pulling down metal bowls and opening and closing the fridge came faintly through.

Dan's explanation made more sense than my fears. "You're probably right."

But there was one other option for who could have been going through our papers. Jarrod could have been looking for evidence that Isabel Addington the cupcake baker was actually his wife Amy Miller.

I didn't want to say it. I didn't want to keep bringing Jarrod up. I didn't want him to still be taking up so much space in my life.

The card for a divorce lawyer that Dan had given me a couple months ago was frayed around the edges from me taking it out of my pocket and turning it over and over in my hands.

I bit back a sigh. Unless I was willing to take the risk of divorcing Jarrod the way Dan wanted—and praying Jarrod didn't kill me as soon as he knew where I was, before I could destroy his reputation—he'd continue to take up space in my world.

I opened my mouth to suggest it was him.

"You're thinking it might have been Jarrod." Dan's words came out before I could form mine.

"Yes," I said softly.

"I don't think he'd take that risk. Not with the trial coming up."

I was a key witness for the prosecution in the trial for Janie's old teacher. The woman had been inappropriate with the children in her care. When Janie spotted her and seemed like she was going to tell someone, her teacher had come up with a plan to kill her and make it look like an allergic reaction. She'd accidentally killed Claire and Dan's grandfather in the process. When I'd figured it out and tried to stop her, she'd tried to kill me as well.

My whole body shuddered. I hadn't been able to keep my name a secret then, and Jarrod had almost found me. Only some skillful lying on Dan's part had kept me safe.

But Jarrod knew I'd have to be at the trial. Amy was a key witness. All he had to do was wait.

Dan was right. Jarrod was too calculating and methodical to risk anything with the trial so close.

Claire had probably moved the papers. Even though she never left a drawer or cupboard open in the house we shared, she could have easily been too tired to notice the drawer here. We were putting in long hours to launch the business and work out the kinks.

"You're right."

"And don't worry about the trial either." Dan's voice was so confident I could almost let my worries go. Almost. "I'm working on a plan to get you in and out of the courtroom in a way that will make it difficult for Jarrod to follow you."

I nodded than remembered he couldn't see me. "Thank you."

"We'll keep you safe. It's going to be okay."

His words had softened and his tone deepened as if he meant more than just the words.

I heard what he wasn't saying. I heard the promise that went beyond the trial.

If I chose to file for divorce, he'd find a way to keep me safe then too.

But he didn't know Jarrod the way I did. The only way to stay safe from Jarrod was to make sure he never found me.

11

Mr. Wendt hadn't matched my mental description of him. The man who opened the door for our visit had a thick, wild thatch of pure white hair on the top of his head. It'd barely even receded. His glasses took up most of his face, and he wore them on a string. But the most surprising thing was he was table leg-thin.

His armchair, however, matched my mental image exactly. The threadbare monstrosity groaned every time he moved.

For the past half hour we'd been discussing the similarities and differences between running a bread bakery and running a cupcake shop.

Mr. Wendt took a second cupcake from the box I'd brought him. I'd included one of everything we'd made for that day. Our cupcake sampler had become one of the most popular items we offered.

I'd been enjoying my visit so much that until he took that second cupcake I'd forgotten part of the reason I'd come. But a second cupcake signaled I'd have to leave soon.

At least with all the shop talk we'd done, the question I'd carefully planned out to lead into what I really wanted to know wouldn't seem so odd.

I shifted on the couch so that I was leaning more in his direction as if curiosity drove me. "If you don't mind me asking, why did you decide to close your shop. It's obvious that you love your business as much as I love mine."

Mr. Wendt nodded his head through my whole question. He set his half-eaten cupcake on a coaster and slid his glasses off. He scrubbed at the lenses with the corner of his sweater as if he couldn't quite look me in the eyes with whatever he was going to say.

My muscles tensed to the point of spasm. Up until my question, Mr. Wendt had been smiling so much I wasn't sure how his cheeks didn't hurt.

Whatever he was about to say was hard for him.

"My wife, she was French." He eased his glasses back up on his face. "That's her there."

He pointed at the wall behind me. I wiggled around in my seat. The picture was a family photo, the kind where a photographer poses you in a configuration that doesn't look at all natural.

A younger Mr. Wendt stood behind a lovely woman with dark hair and dark eyes. One of his hands was on her shoulder. A little girl sat nestled in her lap, and a boy who seemed a fair bit older stood next to his mother.

"She's beautiful."

"Inside as well as out."

The ache in his voice left a dent in my heart. My mother died before I'd been old enough to observe my parents' marriage, but my dad used to have that same sound to his voice when he talked about my mom.

I knew from that alone that Mr. Wendt's wife wasn't around anymore. "How long ago did you lose her?"

"Three years." His tone said he still couldn't believe it'd been that long. "She taught me everything I know about making bread. We worked the store together our whole married life, through two locations and three different landlords."

He paused. I sat in silence with him. I'd give him whatever time he needed. He'd get around to answering my question eventually, and I was in no rush to leave. If he let me, I'd come back and visit him again next week. I couldn't have explained it, but being with Mr. Wendt felt a bit like being with my dad again. They were almost nothing alike. Mr. Wendt hadn't finished high school, and my dad taught English. Mr. Wendt was born in Germany, and my dad had a thread of Cherokee blood.

But there was something about him that made me feel at home.

"I tried working the store after she passed," he finally said.

"But after a while, I just couldn't do it. It wasn't the same once it wasn't a family business anymore."

So his closing up had nothing to do with any increase in crime in the neighborhood. It had a much simpler reason. His heart had left the bakery the day it wasn't something he could do with a person he loved.

The picture he'd pointed out to me had two children in it, though. "Your children weren't interested in continuing the business?"

"My daughter teaches preschool and has two little ones of her own. She loves her job too much to leave it, especially since her hours are the same as the grandkids' school hours." Mr. Wendt buttoned his sweater vest up. His fingers shook slightly. "My son...he started taking an interest in the business right after his mother passed, but...things changed."

The hesitations and gaps in his words were unusual. Everything I'd asked him before—personal or business—had been spoken with the confidence of a man who had nothing to hide. Like a man who enjoyed telling his story to someone and talking shop again.

Now it was almost like he had a secret, and he was too honest a man to know how to hide it.

I didn't know whether to press or not. His son's reasons for leaving the business likely didn't have anything to do with my current problem. It didn't seem right to intrude when it would only be a matter of curiosity. Maybe when Mr. Wendt knew me better, he'd feel comfortable sharing.

He avoided my gaze. If we left the conversation like this, he might not want me to come back, but I didn't know what to say to fix it.

"It's not a secret, Dad."

The man's voice that I'd heard faintly on the other end of the call when I'd reached out to Mr. Wendt about the broken stove came from the doorway.

I turned in my seat. The man in the doorway looked almost like the younger Mr. Wendt in the picture. The only difference was that he had brown eyes instead of Mr. Wendt's blue.

"You can tell her," he said. "It's better than watching you two sit in silence after you've been chattering like squirrels in here for the past hour."

He cast his dad a look that made me think he'd been enjoying hearing his dad talk to me.

The tension seemed to slide off Mr. Wendt in a wave. "I didn't know if…" He trailed off again.

The man shrugged. He lifted a hand at me in greeting. "I'm Flynn. Your question made my dad so uncomfortable because I was in prison. Possession of drugs. I started self-medicating to deal with my grief after my mom died."

His words were so blunt as to sound scripted. They sounded like they'd been copied right out of the mouth of a therapist.

If he'd seen one right away, he likely wouldn't have ended up in prison to begin with, but at least it seemed like he was trying to sort things out now. And he must not have been caught with much in the way of drugs. The sentence for dealing as opposed to possession would have been a lot longer than a couple of years.

I knew what it was like to lose a parent and make bad choices because of it. "I'm sorry, for your loss and for what came after."

He shrugged again. "It was my own fault." He glanced at the box of cupcakes. "You must be the lady who called the other day about the stove."

"I suppose it's not every day you two have to play repairman over the phone."

Flynn chuckled. "I think it brought Dad back to the good-old days. How's it been going since the stove tried to trick you?"

Flynn had such a flippant, laisse-faire attitude that it was hard to see him falling into a depression deep enough that he turned to drugs. But that was the danger of people with certain personalities. Robin Williams was a perfect example. No one would have thought that a lauded comedian would be so depressed that he'd kill himself. It was a good reminder about the importance of looking below the surface and trying to see what people really needed.

The first answer that sprang to my lips in response to Flynn's question was that everything had been going fine. But that would have been one of those answers that allowed people to hide what was bothering them.

Besides, I'd come here to find out if the Wendts had any problems when they rented the space. Just because Mr. Wendt retired due to his wife's death didn't mean they hadn't experienced problems with crime during the time they had the shop. It only meant they hadn't closed up and moved because of it.

I had to know if the vandalism was a community crime and unconnected to the murder—the way Detective Austen thought —or if our shop had been specifically targeted.

"We've actually gotten off to a rocky start. Our landlord was killed and someone vandalized our window all in the same week. Did you ever have problems with crime while you went renting there?"

Mr. Wendt's hands clamped around the ends of his recliner, and he pushed the chair into a full upright position. "No, no problems. It was the best neighborhood. Customers came from the businesses on one side and homes on the other. I felt safe when my wife needed to work there alone."

That disproved the theory that the vandalism was something that was happening in the neighborhood. According to what Mr. Jenner told Claire, the shop wasn't vacant long between Mr. Wendt and when we signed the lease. The safety of the neighborhood couldn't have changed that much in a couple of months, where a murder and a vandalism would happen so close together.

We were somehow the target. Mr. Jenner was dead, but the person who'd killed him might have killed him because Mr.

Jenner surprised them while they were waiting for Claire and me. Either that, or someone had such a grudge against Mr. Jenner that they wanted to continue hurting his heirs even after killing him.

No one would want to kill Claire, which meant either Mr. Jenner was the target or I was. Considering the word that Claire thought had been scrawled on our window was *slut*, Mr. Jenner might have been killed because someone actually wanted to harm me. That sort of derogatory term wasn't generally used for men.

My lungs felt too small to provide me with the oxygen I needed.

"Maybe you shouldn't stay there, my friend," Mr. Wendt said. "It's not the only location for a bakery in this city. I would not want my daughter or my wife working somewhere that two crimes had taken place."

What he didn't understand was that the only person who would want to hurt me was one who would continue to track me no matter where I went. And we couldn't find another location. If we lost this one, we lost the whole business, at least for the next few years. We'd put everything we had into it, and we couldn't afford a more expensive rent.

Mr. Wendt's hands quavered on the arms of his chair. I didn't want to worry him or cause him more stress. Who knew what underlying health conditions he had. If Jarrod had finally found me, frightening Mr. Wendt further over my safety wouldn't make the situation better.

"The new landlord put in security cameras. Hopefully that will at least help scare off whoever's behind this if the neighborhood's no longer being safe."

Mr. Wendt scooted closer to the edge of his chair. "No, no. That's no good. They could hurt you and destroy the recording."

The new owner had thought about any criminal caught on camera wanting to destroy the evidence. "The recording is transmitted off-site. They can't destroy it. Besides, I read somewhere that businesses and homes with security systems are usually passed over by criminals. We should be safe now."

It wasn't a lie. We should be safe if the person who did this was anyone else but Jarrod.

A security system wouldn't deter Jarrod. He'd find some way around it.

Mr. Wendt was shaking his head like he wasn't convinced even by security cameras. He truly must be seeing in Claire and I women who could as easily have been his wife and daughter.

Flynn moved forward and rested a hand on his father's shoulder. "It could be about me."

12

"What do you mean it could be you?" Mr. Wendt's voice shook even more than his hands had been shaking before. "You didn't kill Mr. Jenner. You didn't put paint on Isabel's windows."

Flynn came around and knelt beside Mr. Wendt. He looked up into his face. "I said it could be *about* me. Whoever did this might think you were still renting the shop, and they were trying to get to me through you."

Air rushed into my lungs. This might not be Jarrod. I might not have been the cause of Mr. Jenner's death.

Mr. Wendt's face looked as white as his hair. My relief evaporated.

"Can you explain?" I asked since Mr. Wendt seemed at a loss for words.

Flynn got back to his feet and moved behind his father's

chair again as if he couldn't bear to talk about it while looking Mr. Wendt in the face. "When I got arrested, my dealer couldn't get his money. Now that I'm out, he wants it. He found me and said I needed to pay, but I don't have that kind of cash."

Mr. Wendt moaned. A shudder went over my skin. A dealer wouldn't simply go away because you didn't have the money to pay them. They didn't work off of charity, and they weren't known for being patient.

But Claire and I had nothing to do with Flynn's debt, and neither had Mr. Jenner. "I still don't understand why this would connect to what's been happening to us."

Flynn's shoulders curled forward. "My dealer probably thinks my dad owns the shop and gets money from the rent or is still the one renting the shop. I think he might be trying to create a threatening enough situation that I'll pay him."

"How much?" Mr. Wendt said. "I'll pay whatever he wants to keep you safe."

Flynn jerked slightly and rubbed at the base of his neck. "It's more than you can afford. You'd have to empty your entire retirement savings. I won't take that money from you."

The only sounds in the room were the ticking grandfather clock in the corner and Mr. Wendt's heavy breathing.

I didn't know how much money Mr. Wendt had saved for his retirement, but his home looked fairly comfortable. Flynn must have had a serious addiction over the three years or so that he'd been using. As much as it wouldn't have seemed like it at the time, ending up in prison probably saved him.

Mr. Wendt pressed the heels of his hands to his forehead. "I should have seen it. Your boss, your friends, we all failed you by not seeing it."

Flynn moved close enough again to rest a hand on his father's shoulder. "It's not your fault. It's mine."

It wasn't often that I felt like giving men I'd recently met a hug, but I wished I could give one to Mr. Wendt.

Some people were good liars. Jarrod was one. It seemed like Flynn had been one as well. Maybe being tricked by a good liar didn't make you naïve or stupid or a poor judge of character. Maybe it made you a good person who wanted to think the best of others.

The people who bore the blame for lying and deceiving were the ones doing it. Their victims—like me and Mr. Wendt—shouldn't feel shame over being tricked.

But I couldn't say any of that to Mr. Wendt right now. He'd raised Flynn. It would take him time to understand that once Flynn became an adult, his parents were no longer responsible for his poor choices.

In the meantime, all we could do was try to figure this out and keep Flynn's dealer from continuing to hurt people.

Murder was a big step up from dealing. Some drug dealers were willing to engage in it, but there were likely a lot more who weren't, even when large sums of money were involved. "Is your dealer the kind of guy who'd kill someone?"

Flynn slowly peeled his gaze away from Mr. Wendt and forced it back to me. "I didn't use to think so. He had a reputation for roughing people up but not killing them. Dead guys can't pay." He paused. His gaze shifted to the side. "He might not have meant to kill Mr. Jenner, only to scare him. My dealer's known for breaking bones, a different one each time he comes to collect and you still don't have your money."

I didn't dare look at Mr. Wendt hearing this. In hindsight, Flynn and I should have taken this conversation elsewhere. But we couldn't do that now. Mr. Wendt wouldn't want to be excluded.

My heart felt achingly big watching him listen to his son, his eyes red and his hands running up and down the lengths of his thighs in a self-soothing gesture.

"If they came to 'talk' to Mr. Jenner," Flynn said, "and he resisted, it might have gotten out of control."

So they'd surprised him, Mr. Jenner reacted somehow, and they shot him instead. It was possible. It would have sent a clear message had Mr. Jenner actually been a renter—pay up or we'll start hurting your income until you do.

That seemed almost as backward to me as killing someone who couldn't pay. A man with a damaged business would have a harder time getting the dealer his money.

Then again, so would a man with a broken hand or a broken

leg. Pain motivated, and to avoid it, people would often find a way when it seemed like there hadn't been one before.

I would have wanted to prevent the dealer from continuing his rampage if my only connection had been that I knew and liked Mr. Wendt. But, whoever this dealer was, he'd killed an innocent man and was now targeting my livelihood. Claire and I wouldn't be safe continuing on there if he wasn't stopped.

At the very least, the police needed to look into it, so he could be crossed off the list if we were on the wrong trail. "What's your dealer's name?"

The muscles in Flynn's forearms tensed. "I can't take his name to the police. They'll think I'm still in contact with him. That would violate my probation, and I don't want to go back to jail for the remainder of my sentence."

Something hot and tight burst to life at the base of my throat. Rather than risking violating his parole, he'd put other people in danger? His grief at his mother's death might have been what drove him to drugs, but it seemed like a selfish personality lay at the bottom of it. He still cared about his own pain more than he cared about the pain of the people around him.

"You don't have to talk to the police." I moved my jaw around, convincing my teeth to stop gritting. "I have a friend who's a police detective. I'll slip him the name, and no one will know it came from you."

Flynn rubbed a finger along the side of his nose, and then his gaze drifted to his dad. "I can't take that risk. If it got back to my dealer, he might come for my dad directly. I can't risk that. Not without proof that this has something to do with my debt."

The heat in my chest waned. If my dad were still alive, I'd want to protect him too. After all, I'd left Fair Haven and had very little interaction with my friend Nicole because I didn't want Jarrod hurting her to get information about me. I couldn't fault Flynn for doing what I had essentially done.

But that still left us with a major problem. Mr. Wendt sat up in his chair, his back as straight as his age would allow. "You need to tell her, Flynn. She and her business partner are innocent in all this."

"I can't without more proof." Flynn's gaze shifted to the ceiling, as if he were thinking. "I'll come hang around the shop. That won't seem suspicious if he thinks my dad's still involved with the place. If I see anyone associated with my dealer, then it'll be worth the risk of giving you his name."

13

The bakery was still empty other than the woman working on her computer when I got back from the post office. I hadn't been sure about leaving Scott alone, but he'd assured me that he could handle it. Besides, this time of the morning, we always had a slow stretch where we rarely had more than one customer in the bakery. Since I'd wanted to go make sure all mail would be sent to the bakery from now on, it'd seemed like the ideal opportunity to step out.

Scott wasn't at the counter when I came in. That was a little odd, but he'd probably just quickly gone to the restroom. I couldn't begrudge him that.

I stripped off my jacket and headed for my office to hang it up. I pushed open the door.

Scott straightened up from behind my desk. He smiled at me

as if nothing were out of the ordinary. "Did you get your errand done?" His voice was light.

He shouldn't have been in my office. We didn't assign him any work that would have required it. But he was acting like nothing was amiss.

The memory of the misplaced papers and slightly ajar desk drawer gnawed at the back of my mind. What reason would Scott have for going through my desk drawers? He knew we didn't keep any money in there. Besides, if he wanted money, he had access to the cash register. He could have emptied it and taken off before now.

If he were doing something he shouldn't be, I didn't want him to know I was suspicious. Worry about someone being out front for customers was a reasonable excuse. He obviously hadn't heard me come in after all.

I dropped my coat on the hook. "All taken care of. What are you doing in here? You might not hear a customer come in."

"I was looking for another pen." He held up one of the pens from the box I kept in the desk drawer. "The one we usually keep up front for phone orders is AWOL."

That made sense. Everything that was happening, along with the court case I'd soon have to testify in and the chance that Jarrod would find me because of it, had me suspecting every-thing. And everyone.

Scott hadn't given me any other reason to suspect him. In

fact, he'd been a model employee, working almost as hard as Claire and I did.

I grinned at him. And at my own silliness. "Maybe we ought to tie it down this time. Or I should order some with our company name on it. That way, if they sprout legs, at least we get some free publicity."

THE OLD-FASHIONED BELL WE'D HUNG ABOVE THE BAKERY DOOR jangled, and Dan waved to me. The look on his face and the fact that he was here during the work day said this wasn't just a surprise pleasure visit.

He was here because of what I'd told him after my conversation with Flynn and Mr. Wendt.

Dan stopped in front of the counter. "I'd ask what's good, but I know it all is."

He glanced around the shop. It was the middle of the afternoon, so only one table was occupied.

"Can you slip away?" He lowered his voice. "I have something I want to talk to you about, but this isn't the place."

Normally I wouldn't have been able to. Today was Claire's day off. But Scott had shown up this morning asking if he could get more hours. I hadn't had the heart to turn him away, especially since we still needed to get his social security number for tax purposes.

"Let me just grab my jacket and tell Scott that I'm stepping out."

In Florida, this would have been one of the nicest times of the year. The heat would have let up, but the dampness that sometimes came in the winter wouldn't have set in yet. Tourists would be filling up all the hotels and resorts in the major cities.

Michigan weather had already turned colder than Florida in January even though it was only late October. The weather was one of the few things I missed about my old home.

Dan led the way toward the park down the street. The leaves were a riot of sunset colors. It would have been a romantic place to walk had we been dating.

Part of me wanted to talk to him again about why I couldn't file for divorce. But he'd already heard all the reasons. He felt that we could protect me from Jarrod even once he knew where I was.

He wouldn't be so sure if he'd ever met my husband.

We turned into the park. The paths were empty.

Dan's head swiveled around as if he were making sure. "I looked into Flynn Wendt's arrest record. He pled guilty and didn't even try going to trial. Unfortunately, he also refused to give up his dealer's name, even though the district attorney offered him a shorter sentence in exchange for the information."

He could have gotten a drug dealer off the street and been out of jail faster himself, but he'd chosen not to do it? "I don't understand why he'd make that choice."

Dan's hand accidentally brushed against mine. My heart torqued painfully in my chest. If there were no Jarrod, we could be walking hand in hand. If there were no murder and no vandalism, this could have been a visit Dan made just because he missed me and wanted to see me.

And if wishes were horses, I'd be running a prize breeding stable right now instead of a bakery. Wishing for what I didn't have—couldn't have—wasn't going to make me feel better. It certainly wasn't going to solve this case.

Dan was watching my face as if he wasn't sure how much to say. I'd seen him wear that expression before when he wanted to protect me.

"I'd rather know the truth, even if it's scary."

That had always been my motto, and it'd kept me alive so far.

Dan nodded. "It was Flynn's first offense. He had no prior record. He never came to work high, according to the character reference his boss wrote. He never drove high as far as we can tell. His sentence wasn't going to be a long one, and with good behavior, he was obviously going to be eligible for parole in even less time."

Something in Dan's voice shifted, and I glanced up at him.

His expression was somber. "If he'd given up his dealer, he might not have come out alive. Snitches tend to have short lifespans in jail."

It still seemed selfish, but it also made sense. I couldn't be sure I wouldn't have made the same choice. Self-preservation instincts were strong in most people.

But that meant we couldn't find out the name of Flynn's dealer through his records the way Dan and I had hoped when I'd called him. Dan had taken the risk of looking into a case that didn't belong to him, and it hadn't even yielded results.

"Do you have any guesses for who his dealer might be?" I asked.

The wind gusted past, and a handful of leaves from the tree right in front of us twirled down.

Dan stayed silent, but I had the feeling it wasn't because he hadn't heard my question. He just wasn't sure how much he wanted to tell me.

I didn't blame him. My track record for staying out of things and staying safe wasn't good. Even when I tried to be careful, I ended up in the middle of it, as if I were a strong magnet and trouble was metal fragments.

"Assuming Flynn was buying from someone in the neighborhood, there's one very likely candidate. A man by the name of Edgar Serranno."

"His turf is around the bakery?" I wasn't sure *turf* was the right word. Jarrod hadn't worked narcotics, and my upbringing with an English professor father had been focused more on ancient literature than modern events.

"He controls the drugs sales in a large section of town that covers where the bakery is," Dan said, "where Mr. Wendt lives, and where Flynn used to work. All the minor dealers get their product from him and owe him a cut of their profits."

That Flynn wouldn't give the name to the police after his arrest still made sense. Snitching could have gotten him killed. But refusing to give *me* the name hadn't served any purpose except to cost us time.

Though, we didn't have evidence to tell us who Flynn meant when he talked about his dealer. Edgar Serranno might not be the one directly involved. It could have been one of his minions.

"If it was that easy to figure out who controlled the area, I don't understand why Flynn wouldn't give me the name."

Dan drew in a long, slow breath and let it out with equal care. "If the person behind this is Serranno, it doesn't surprise me that Flynn doesn't want to even speak his name."

I shivered despite the fact that my coat was plenty warm enough for the fall afternoon. I nodded to let Dan know I still wanted him to continue.

"About a year ago, Serranno was the main suspect in the deaths of a couple of teenagers. He'd started selling a dangerous new cocktail. The department and the district attorney thought they finally had him because the friend of the two teens who died was willing to testify. He went missing before he could."

So much for Flynn's belief that his drug dealer wouldn't kill anyone. He might have meant the individual dealer he bought from rather than the man in charge. I couldn't believe Flynn didn't know a drug lord was capable of murder if he was too frightened to say his name.

Flynn seemed to want to help, but not at the risk of himself or his dad. Which meant that I couldn't fully trust him. He'd help Claire and me only so far as he felt safe.

That might still get us farther than we could get without his help. If he could identify an associate of Edgar Serranno watching the store or even coming into the store, we'd know we were on the right track.

I just couldn't expect Flynn to stick his neck out for us if it came to that.

We turned around and headed back for the bakery. "Do we need to...should we tell Claire about this?"

Dan looked down at me, and his expression made my breath catch in my throat. The look said I was special. All I'd done was care about Claire, and yet he looked at me like I was special.

His fingers grazed mine. It could have been an accident, but I was sure it wasn't. If only we didn't have to confine it to a quick touch. Right now, I could have used the security of holding his hand.

"I think we have to tell Claire." Dan's voice was somber. "If Serranno is behind this, neither of you are safe alone at the shop after dark."

14

*D*an's warning about Edgar Serranno and what he was capable of had me looking both ways even though it was ten o'clock in the morning on a Monday. If the drug dealer had evaded arrest—or, at least, evaded having a charge stick—for as long as it sounded, then he wouldn't risk doing anything when people were out on the street. I hoped not anyway. Mr. Jenner had been killed sometime around seven in the morning, and that only a few hours earlier than now.

Maybe I should have accepted Claire's offer to come with me. It'd just seemed unfair to drag her in on the one day we were closed because I'd forgotten the tools I used to make gum paste flowers and had promised Janie a lesson after school. Coming with me would have meant Claire couldn't get her bike ride in before her brunch date with a few of the female cousins who were closer to her age. She'd been looking forward to both, especially since fall in Michigan could be unpredictable.

Besides, we didn't even know if Flynn's drug dealer was the one targeting the store. We wouldn't know until Flynn started hanging around later this week in between his job interviews.

I lifted my chin and marched from the car to the door. I jammed my key into the lock and turned.

No resistance. No click signaling the lock had turned.

The door wasn't locked?

That couldn't be right. I was the last one out. Claire had already been waiting for me in the car. No way could I have forgotten to lock up.

But I had been rushing, not wanting to keep Claire waiting. I'd forgotten my tools for that very reason.

The muscles in my shoulders felt so tight that moving my arms hurt. How could I have been so stupid? With everything that was going on, to forget to lock the door was unpardonable.

I pulled the door open and stepped inside. From now on, I'd have to make a habit of double checking that the door was locked before I left. I never would have been so careless when I'd been living in my truck. Every moment of my life had been about safeguards and back-up plans. Letting some of that go was healthy, but I needed to make sure I didn't go so far as to neglect common caution.

I headed for the kitchen.

A rustling noise like papers blowing in the wind came from the office.

I froze. The office didn't have a window, and I knew I hadn't left papers out on the desk this time. After the time I'd thought things had been moved around, I'd made a point of putting everything away at the end of each day.

Was someone in there?

The sound had been so soft that I might have imagined it... except the door had been unlocked as well.

I needed to call Dan. I wasn't going to call 9-1-1 without proof someone was in there. I'd have to give them my name.

I dialed Dan's number. He didn't pick up. The call went to voice mail, and I hung up. If I even whispered a message, the person in the other room—if someone was really in there—might hear me. Dan might not check his messages for hours, and then I'd have given away my presence with no back-up coming.

Whoever was here hadn't come out yet, and they must have heard me come in. Since I'd used the front door, the bell had rung upon my entry.

Maybe I could use that to my advantage to keep them in there until I could reach Dan. The office door didn't lock, so I'd have to think of something else.

The chairs set up around the tables caught my gaze. I had no idea if wedging a chair under a doorknob actually worked, but it was worth a try.

All I had to do was move quietly enough that they didn't

know what I was doing. If they figured out I was trying to trap them, they'd probably risk letting me see them in order to make a break for it.

I edged backward toward the nearest table and wrapped my hands around the chair back. I lifted it. My arm and shoulder muscles burned. Why had we chosen such heavy chairs?

I shuffled as soundlessly as possible across the room, toward my office door.

I was halfway there when the doorknob started to turn.

The movement was so slow that I wouldn't have noticed it if I hadn't been watching the door as intently as a cat waiting for a mouse to emerge from its hole.

Except I was definitely not the predator in this situation.

And I had nowhere to go. I couldn't reach either the kitchen or the front door in time. My only weapon was the chair, and it was getting heavier by the second.

The door opened, its hinges creaking because we'd run out of time to oil them.

A pause.

And then Scott's head poked out. His gaze scanned the room and landed on me.

"Isabel!" His voice came out in a squawk. His skin had a pasty tone that made freckles I hadn't noticed before stand out on his cheeks. "What are you doing here?"

I lowered the chair, but I didn't move out from behind it. At the very least, I could knock it down in front of him if I had to make a run for it. All the times I'd thought Scott was odd came rushing back to me.

Scott knew we were closed on Mondays. "What are you doing here?" My voice came out cautious and slow.

Blotches of pink stained his cheeks. "You, uhh, you'd been asking for my social security number and other stuff for taxes. I came to fill in the paperwork." He straightened up as if he hadn't been trying to peek out of the office to see if the room was clear only a moment before. "When I heard a noise, I thought it might have been whoever killed your landlord coming back."

My heart rate dropped a notch, but Fear still rattled at his cage in the back of my mind. "How did you get in?"

He shrugged. It almost looked natural. "The door was unlocked."

That almost made sense. Claire would have believed him. Most people would have believed him.

Except for one thing. He couldn't have known the door would be unlocked. No one came to a place that should be locked and just hoped someone would have forgotten to lock it.

Scott must have picked the lock. He must have been the one who killed Mr. Jenner. But then why spray paint nasty words on our windows and help clean it off afterward? Why stick around? And why break into my office again today?

We stared at each other.

I gripped the back of the chair. What did I do here? If I told him I was calling the police, he'd have no reason to stick around.

I didn't have a gun or anything else over him. For all I knew, Scott wasn't even his real name.

But if I let him go, he could come back and hurt us later. His picture might not even be on the security cameras. Since he worked here, he'd probably figured out any blind spots.

I edged one hand toward the pocket where my phone was.

Scott stepped back across the office threshold. "What are you doing? We can talk about this."

I stopped, hand halfway to my pocket. His hands were extended slightly out in front of him as if he wasn't sure whether to put them in the air or use them as a shield.

He was afraid of me.

That made even less sense. Why would he be afraid of me... unless he wasn't the one who did those things?

I slowly put my hand back on the chair, but I kept my gaze firmly on him in case this was a trick. "How did you really get in here?"

Scott moved his hand toward his pocket.

"Stop!" My voice didn't sound much steadier than his. I pretended as if I was going to reach for whatever weapon he thought I had. "If I can't go for what's in my pocket, then neither can you."

Scott actually raised his hands this time. "It's just a key. I have a key."

We hadn't given him a key. "Only Claire and I have a key. Did you steal hers? Or make a copy when we weren't watching?"

Scott's eyebrows dipped slightly, and he lowered his hands. "I have a key of my own."

I'd preferred it when his hands were in the air. He didn't look as frightened of me anymore. "I'm going to call the police."

He took a step out of the doorway. "Do you think I'm here to hurt you?"

I had to keep the chair between us. I had to make sure he didn't get between me and the door. "I don't know why you're here, or why you did any of the other things you did, but that's why we're going to call the police to sort it out. So don't come any closer."

His eyebrows scrunched down fully this time. "What other things?"

He had to be kidding. Like he didn't know exactly what had gone on here.

My brain slowed slightly, like an anxious person taking a deep breath. He'd looked scared of me when he'd discovered me here. As scared as I felt.

A hardened criminal who'd killed and vandalized wouldn't look that frightened, even if they felt it.

Something wasn't right here. The fact that he'd been avoiding giving us any other information about himself than his first name flashed like a beacon in my mind.

"Who are you really?"

He met my gaze. "Scott Jenner. Robert Jenner was my father."

15

I hadn't met Bob Jenner, so I couldn't see a family resemblance. Scott could still be lying to me.

"I have a key," he was saying, "because this is my property now. I'm his only child, and he and my mom divorced when I was five."

Were those too many details? I couldn't remember what Jarrod used to say about people who were lying—whether their stories were too vague or whether they added in a lot of detail hoping it would make their story sound true.

"If you're our new landlord, why not just say so? Why pretend you needed a job? Why come in here when we're closed?"

Scott didn't flinch at the questions, look away, or give any other sign that he didn't know how to answer them.

"I thought the police were wrong when they told me you and

Claire didn't have anything to do with my dad's death. Especially once I came by to check the place out and found the spray paint on the windows. It seemed like you might be running some sort of scam or insurance fraud."

So he'd pretended to be a kid looking for work to save for college in order to find evidence. "You're not actually saving up for college, are you?"

He shook his head. "I'm twenty-two. I already graduated with a business degree."

If he was telling the truth, then it explained something else as well. "You've searched my office more than once."

It was more of a statement than a question. Scott had to be the one who'd moved the papers before.

He crossed his arms but didn't make any move to come closer. "Yes."

At least it was good to know that Detective Austen didn't suspect us anymore. Or, at least, she'd told Scott we weren't people of interest.

It was also good to know that I wasn't imagining things. I knew those papers had been moved.

"I almost didn't come in today." Scott shrugged his shoulders up high and let them drop like he was rolling a heavy weight off them. "The longer I've worked with you and Claire, the more convinced I was that you hadn't killed my dad. I just wasn't sure yet that you weren't trying to run some other kind of scam. But everything in your paperwork is legitimate, and you didn't even file an insurance claim for the vandalism. You were going to pay me out-of-pocket for cleaning it up."

I would have felt insulted that he thought we might be criminals and murderers if I hadn't suspected innocent people myself before. "You thought we might be running a scam even though Claire's cousin is a police officer?"

Scott's ears turned red. "I thought that's why the police didn't suspect you."

Nepotism wasn't unheard of, but Dan wasn't the kind of person who'd ask other officers to overlook a crime for him. The farthest he'd gone was to ask Detective Austen not to request my real name, and he had legitimate reasons for that. "Detective Austen didn't play any favors. She treated me like I was a suspect every time I talked to her."

Scott came out of the office door and stood at the end of the counter. "Are you going to fire me now?"

He could still be playing me, but I didn't think so. I moved the chair back where it belonged. "If you were only here to figure out if we killed your dad, why do you want to stay?"

"I moved back here to start working with my dad a couple weeks before he died, and the rest of my family lives across the country." Scott rubbed behind his ear, as if this was more embarrassing than anything he'd already had to admit to. "I don't have any friends here yet. What else am I going to do with my time while I'm waiting for the lawyers to settle the estate so I can actually manage my new business?"

The space inside my chest felt too small for my heart again. Claire would probably tell me that I needed to stop empathizing with everyone who had even the smallest similarity with me. But I knew what it was like to be in a new town with no one. You felt like no one would miss you if you disappeared. No one liked to feel that way. No one liked to feel like they didn't have anyone to call if they got sick or needed help.

"I'm not going to fire you. I wouldn't even if you weren't our new landlord."

Scott smiled. It crinkled his cheeks and made him look much younger than his twenty-two years. I really couldn't be blamed for believing his story given how young he looked.

He dipped his head. "Thank you. You and Claire didn't do this, but this shop is still the only link I have. I call the police station every day. Detective Austen keeps telling me there's nothing new in the case, which means they have no idea who hurt my dad. I'm afraid my dad's murder won't ever be solved."

"Do you want to see what I've dug up so far? Maybe if we work together, we can figure it out."

16

I brewed a fresh pot of coffee to share with Scott. We didn't have any day-old snacks. Since we were closed Mondays, I took anything that didn't sell on Sunday to the local homeless shelter. Even though our funds were tight, we had so much more than the people who used the shelter did.

And I'd lived in their world for a short time. A few baked goods wouldn't get them a job or help them overcome an addiction. What it could do was show them they weren't invisible. It could bring a tiny spot of joy into a day that probably hadn't allowed much room for hope.

I updated Scott on how we thought the vandalism and the murder could be related, what I'd learned from Flynn Wendt, and what Dan told me about the drug lord who controlled the neighborhood.

Scott wrapped both hands around his coffee cup, his shoulders slouched forward. "I guess it's better thinking my dad was in the wrong place at the wrong time than that he'd done something to get himself killed."

I'm not sure I would have found the same comfort in that. Then my loved one's death would feel random and purposeless. "That's only one theory. Flynn's going to hang around here for a few days to see if he recognizes anyone."

Scott's gaze shot up from his cup. The skin around his eyes was red. "That's a bad idea. If he's able to recognize someone, they'll recognize him as well. It'll reinforce the idea that his family is still connected to the shop."

I hadn't thought of that. The last thing we needed was Edgar Serranno putting even more pressure on us because he thought we were working for the Wendts. "I'll call Flynn and let him know not to come."

"Maybe he'd be willing to watch a few hours of the security footage to see if he recognizes anyone that way."

The security cameras only watched a limited area, basically both doors and the cash register. They also weren't on during the day when customers were coming in and out. They turned on with the alarm system. But it was better than nothing. If the drug lord had assigned someone to keep an eye on us, he might have been caught on camera when we were closing down the shop at night.

"Any other theories?" Scott asked.

I shook my head.

He refilled both our cups and sat back down. He didn't drink from his right away.

"It has to be an accident. My dad…" He shook his head. "I know what people say about rich landlords. They think they're all about the money, but my dad wasn't like that. He grew up poor. He knew what it was like. He made deals no one else would make, gave people chances."

He gave us one. It didn't surprise me that he also made arrangements with others.

"You can't think of anyone who might want to hurt him?" I asked.

Scott stared at the wall behind me as if thinking it through then shook his head.

To figure this out I needed a better picture of who his dad was. Maybe Scott's perception of his dad wasn't the full picture. "Why did your parents' divorce?"

Scott stirred his coffee. The fact that he hadn't reacted by getting defensive told me that he understood I wasn't accusing his mom of flying out here and killing his dad.

Scott swung his spoon back and forth, letting it dangle from his fingers above the cup. "Money. Though both my parents tell it a different way. My mom said my dad was too controlling and never let her do what she wanted. My dad said my mom spent without considering the consequences, and it was sabotaging his ability to build the kind of business and life that he wanted."

Arguments over money ranked number one among married

couples. Whenever it came up, it showed me how unusual my marriage had been once again. I hadn't even had a credit card. What money I got, I had to ask Jarrod for, like a child begging her parents for an allowance. He hadn't let me work. He'd wanted me home, taking care of things there so that he didn't have to do anything when he finished work for the day. The longer we were married, the less he allowed me out of the house. Shortly before I left, he'd even started grocery shopping with me or going himself with a list I made.

Scott's spoon stopped swinging. He balanced it across the top of the cup. "My dad says he fought to keep me, but the courts always favor the wife, especially back then. So my dad paid child support, and I stayed with him in the summers, learning his business practically before I could do division or multiplication."

And then he'd gone on to business school and graduated, excited to finally be an official part of his dad's business and play a bigger role in his dad's life only to have this happen. So often life didn't seem fair.

Bob Jenner didn't sound like the kind of man who would have made a lot of enemies. At least, he didn't sound like a man who would have made a lot of enemies among the average people.

"Is there anyone at all who you can think of who might have had a reason to harm your dad? We need to figure out if this was about him or not."

"I know everyone says this when they lose someone through

a tragedy, but I really can't. My dad helped people build a better life. He didn't rent gouge."

Claire had never explained to me why Mr. Jenner had been willing to make the unusual deal with us that he did. That explained it. He was a business man, but he was also a man who wanted to see other people succeed in life. It wasn't the most secure business plan, but it was a way to go to bed content at night. "Was there anyone who'd benefit financially from his death?"

Scott gave a shrug-head shake combo. "Only me. He left everything to me."

Given Scott had worked here undercover because he suspected we'd killed his father, he wasn't a good suspect. The plans he'd had for his future were upended when they'd barely started.

Maybe that was it. "Did a lot of people know that you planned to come back after school and work in your dad's business so that you could carry on even once he retired?"

"Only my parents and a few of my friends from school. Why?"

That meant that whoever killed Bob Jenner probably thought that the family would sell off his properties rather than continuing to maintain them. Mr. Jenner might have been appreciated and loved by the people he helped, but he likely wasn't as popular among those who would have liked to take advantage of the people he helped. Someone also might have seen the prime real estate Mr. Jenner controlled—like our bakery —going to "waste" when it could have been earning so much more.

"What if someone killed your dad because they wanted to buy this property, and he wouldn't sell it to them? It would explain the vandalism too. Making the neighborhood seem unsafe would motivate whoever inherited to sell more quickly and cheaply."

Scott pulled out his cell phone. "The property isn't listed with a Realtor. I didn't plan to sell. If anyone wanted it, they probably spoke to Dad's lawyer, and he turned them away."

He tapped the button for speakerphone and set his phone on the table.

I recognized the receptionist's voice and the hold music from when I'd tried to speak to Bob Jenner's lawyer about contacting next of kin.

"Did you tell your lawyer not to give us your contact information?"

Scott dropped his gaze. "I called him right after I heard you and Claire talking about it. I didn't want you knowing who I was."

We'd been lucky that Scott was on our side. We'd taken him in without enough questions or enough care because he seemed honest and young and in need of a job. Had he been a mole for Edgar Serranno or someone else unethical, we would have been in trouble.

I'd always thought I was suspicious and paranoid and careful. Turned out I had a blind spot like everyone else. When I saw someone who seemed lost, I wanted to take them in.

The lawyer answered, and Scott explained what we were looking for.

"There was one inquiry," the lawyer said. "Let me look it up for you in my notes."

The sound of computer keys clicking filled the air. "Here it is. Edwardo Sharp. He's called three times."

"Did you write down the dates of those calls?"

More clicking. "They were all after your father passed. He wanted to know if the heir had decided what to do with the property yet. I told him you intended to keep it. As per your instructions, I didn't give him your information."

Scott and I exchanged a glance over the phone. Scott trying to hide from us might have saved his life if we were right. For all we knew, the man who wanted to buy the property was also the one who'd killed his father. Scott might have been next if he refused to sell too.

I mimed for Scott to mute his cell phone so that his lawyer couldn't hear for a moment. "I think you should set up a meeting with Edwardo Sharp to talk about selling the property. It would give us a chance to meet him and see if he might be behind all this."

Scott unmuted the phone without any hesitation. "I'll need whatever phone number he left."

17

I plated two cupcakes and handed them across to the woman who'd finished paying Scott at the register. "Are you sure you don't mind staying to help Claire? I feel bad because we're not paying you."

"Send me home with another box of leftovers at the end of the day, and we'll call it even." He cast a smile in my direction. "I have a second date tonight, so I was going to buy a sampler anyway. I think an outdoor picnic with cupcakes and coffee is the perfect thing. It's warm today."

Based on the way he was grinning and trying not to, he had it bad. Hopefully the second date led to a third one. Not that I wasn't grateful for his help. I was. But a young man like him needed friends his own age.

I turned for my office. "I shouldn't be gone more than a few hours anyway."

At least, that's what Dan had said. He'd be picking me up any minute to drive me to a restaurant where he'd reserved a private room for me to meet with the prosecutor in the case against Janie's former teacher, Ms. Glover. As hard as the prosecution had tried to build a solid case without my testimony, they hadn't been able to.

So, for two hours today, I had to be Amy Miller. And because Amy Miller had an abusive husband who wanted to see her dead, Dan had decided it'd be safer to meet the prosecutor at a neutral location. If Jarrod were watching the prosecutor's office, he wouldn't see me enter. He also wouldn't see her go someplace where a meeting of this kind would normally take place. The prosecutor would go to a restaurant, where Dan and I would already be waiting. That way, if Jarrod decided to wait and see if I showed up to meet with her, he'd never know I was there.

I slid into my desk chair and spread out the supply orders that I wanted to approve before I had to leave.

Two sharp raps came on my door frame. Dan was early. Time to face whatever the prosecutor had in store for me. Since she'd be prepping me to withstand cross-examination, it likely wouldn't be a fun experience.

I forced the smile I always thought of as my soldier-going-to-war-smile, the smile of someone proud to be doing their duty, while simultaneously being scared and not wanting to let on to the people they cared about how scared they were.

I looked up. Flynn stood in the door where I'd expected to find Dan.

Flynn gestured behind him at the main part of the store. "The kid at the counter said I could come in."

The "kid" at the counter wouldn't have said that if he'd known who Flynn was.

I stood. "Didn't you get my voicemail?"

"I got it." Flynn came into the office and took the only other chair. "I still think it's worth the risk if we can catch who did this, don't you?"

On one hand, yes. We'd all be safer in the long-term once the police were able to arrest the person behind the murder and vandalism.

On the other hand, even if Flynn was able to identify someone, it didn't guarantee an arrest. The police couldn't charge a person for walking this street or even coming into my shop. Yes, it would confirm who was likely behind all this, but Scott didn't think that was worth the risk. As the owner of this shop and my soon-to-be-landlord, I had to respect that even if he did look like a teenager.

I went back to my chair but stayed standing. Hopefully Flynn would see that my words and my body language matched. "I'm not the sole decision-maker here. It was a good idea, but we're going to have to hope the video footage caught something."

Flynn rubbed his hands slowly up and down the arm rests of the chair, a move that echoed what his father did when upset.

"The thing is I was actually hoping this might turn into you hiring me." He glanced back at the open door as if he was embarrassed to have anyone else hear him. "I tried to get a job in my field. No one will hire me because of my history. Now I just need a job, any job."

That plea would have been hard enough to turn down if I hadn't met and liked his father. How could I face Mr. Wendt again if I refused to help his son when I could?

And yet, now wasn't the time, for more reasons than that we couldn't have Flynn seen around the shop.

"We don't have the money or shifts for another employee right now, but you'll be the first person I'll call when we do."

Flynn's eyebrows moved into a straight line, and his eyes hardened around the edges. He clearly thought it was a brush-off.

"I mean it," I said. "Scott at the counter is only temporary, and we'll need extra hands for the holiday rush, okay?"

Flynn's smile returned, but it didn't reach his eyes. "Yeah, sure."

I couldn't really blame him for not believing me. Many of the people he'd interviewed with had probably made him similar promises just to get rid of him. A criminal record was never something employers went looking for. For many of them, the risk was too great. Even in a case like Flynn's, where it'd been a drug possession charge rather than theft or a violent crime, employers probably worried about him being unreliable. He wouldn't reach the point in the consideration process where potential employers checked his references and found out he was reliable even while on drugs. Many people had heard of functional alcoholics. I'd never heard of a functional drug addict, so it wasn't surprising that Flynn was struggling for work.

I knew the challenges of trying to rebuild your life after you'd done something you regretted. Maybe there was something we could do to help in the future, but we couldn't right now. I couldn't let my blind spot allow me to make another potentially foolish decision.

I moved to the doorway. Hopefully he'd get the hint. Dan would be here any minute now.

Flynn swiveled in his chair but didn't relinquish it. "What if I came in after hours and did janitorial work? No one would see me then."

That was definitely a place where we could use help. Having someone come in and take care of the day's mess would mean we could both get more sleep and focus on baking.

Dan appeared in the doorway. "Ready to go?"

I went back to my chair and grabbed my jacket. I turned to Flynn. He still wasn't showing any signs of getting up. "I'll talk to my business partner and see what we can do."

Flynn glanced at Dan. I couldn't see if Dan gave him a firm look or if Dan's bearing said *I'm a cop* regardless of his plain clothes attire, but Flynn got to his feet.

"I appreciate you considering it," Flynn said to me.

He ducked past us both and left. Hopefully Edgar Serranno didn't have someone stationed to watch the shop 24/7. If he did, Flynn's innocent drop by could cause us a lot more trouble.

THE SLIGHT HOLD-UP WITH FLYNN MEANT THAT DAN AND I didn't have to wait long until the prosecuting attorney showed up at the restaurant. Watching her walk into the room felt like a force of nature had entered in a human body. She was probably fifteen years my senior with close-cropped silver hair and a look that could have been put together by a professional stylist.

Claire had chosen my clothes that morning. She'd put me in one of the outfits she'd bought for me when I'd had to suddenly move into her home to avoid a health code violation for living in my truck. I planned to let her pick out my outfit for the trial as well. Claire had a much better sense of what would give the right impression than I did. I definitely wanted the jury to see me as a reliable witness rather than as a woman who'd been essentially homeless and broke at the time when I'd stopped Janie's teacher from killing her.

The prosecutor shook Dan's hand first. "Always a pleasure, Detective Holmes."

Her voice had more gravel in it than I was used to hearing from a woman.

She turned icy blue eyes on me. "I'm Anna Hall, and you must be Mrs. Miller."

The name hit me like I shove. I flinched. It was like someone had stripped away everything I'd become in the past two years and sent me back to the shell of a person I'd been. I could almost hear Jarrod laughing at me, asking me why I thought I could ever get away.

"Well," Anna tilted her head to one side, reminding me of an eagle surveying a rabbit, "there's your first bit of homework. You can't recoil every time the defense uses your name."

I nodded. My voice had temporarily fled.

Anna gestured for us to take a seat. Dan pulled out my chair for me like some old-school gentleman. He settled his chair slightly closer to mine than was technically necessary. Not close enough to make anyone suspicious, but close enough that I felt like I had an ally. Technically, Anna Hall was my ally too, but today's meeting was about preparing me. By the end, she'd likely feel like an enemy.

Anna's penetrating gaze fell on me again. "That actually brings up the biggest challenge we're going to face. You're the key witness against Ms. Glover, and so the defense will try to discredit you in any way they can."

My teeth clenched against my will. I had to do this. I had to do it for Janie and for every other child that Ms. Glover had hurt. As long as I stayed focused on my reason for doing this, I could make it through.

Anna pulled a small laptop out of her bag. "I need to make sure you've told me everything that could be used against you, so I can help you be ready for it when the defense drags it out to use as a weapon."

She didn't sound like she thought highly of defense attorneys. Based on what Nicole had told me about why she almost left her profession and why she only represents people she believes are innocent, Anna wasn't far off the mark.

She was looking at me as if she expected me to start my list. What kinds of things did most people talk about? Not every crappy thing people did could be used to discredit them in court.

"I used to live in my truck," I said. My words came out soft and choppy.

"What was that?"

I cleared my throat. "I used to live in my truck. I was homeless."

She typed that into her laptop. "That shouldn't cause us too much trouble. The fact that you now live at a permanent address and run a business suggests you have a hardworking, forthright character. You turned your life around. Besides, I assume they'd have trouble proving that?"

Dan shifted beside me. "It'd be next to impossible. I didn't even realize at the time. Mrs. Miller didn't share that information, for obvious reasons."

Hearing Dan call me Mrs. Miller made my stomach feel queasy. Did the words taste as bad on his lips coming out?

"Next?" Anna prompted.

I hadn't done anything else wrong. I even paid taxes, albeit through my incorporated business. I shook my head and shrugged.

She moved her laptop to the side so that there wasn't a barrier between us anymore. "There's no point in avoiding this. As I see it, our biggest potential problem is your husband. Detective Holmes has filled me in on the basics, but I need to know how vindictive he might be."

How vindictive? How was I even supposed to answer that? I'd had to sneak out of the house with only what I could carry, and then I had to disappear. I'd become someone else. "He tried to kill me the first time he found me. He will kill me if he gets the opportunity."

"That I already knew." She looked at Dan and did this thing with her face where her entire expression seemed to lift in question. "I believe the police department is working on protection for you."

"That's correct," Dan said.

She shifted back to face me. "So what I'm really asking is would your husband derive any personal benefit from perjuring himself to call into question your character?"

My mouth went so dry that I wished this had actually been a lunch date. At least then I would have had a glass of water.

Jarrod would have no problem getting on the stand and telling everyone that I was a liar. That I was unstable. Doing so would align with his purposes perfectly. If I ever tried to speak out about what he'd done to me, he'd have already testified in court, under oath, that I was a liar.

My lungs felt like they collapsed. I couldn't get enough air. "The defense might call Jarrod as a character witness against me?"

Anna looked like she wanted to pat my hand but that she also knew coddling me now would only harm me later. "It's a possibility we need to be ready for."

18

"I have a problem."

Claire stood just inside my office door. We weren't technically closed for another twenty minutes, but we hadn't had a customer for over half an hour. I'd taken the opportunity to brainstorm some new cupcake flavor ideas.

My mind was not in the right space for problems. At least, not for the kind that usually found us.

Claire's face was pinched and her hands were on her hips, both sure signs that she was frustrated. "I forgot to pick up the antibiotic drops for my ear. If I don't go right now, I won't make it before they close."

I felt like I should blink and shake my head to clear the cobwebs. That didn't seem like a problem. A problem would be she'd found a stash of illegal weapons at the back of the freezer or rats in the pantry.

"I'm just so angry at myself for forgetting," Claire said.

I got to my feet. "Go now."

Claire's gaze flickered between me and the door. "Dan doesn't want us here alone after dark."

Hence the problem. I should have seen that from the start.

But someone would have to be watching the shop constantly for this to be a problem. It wasn't a pattern. One of us wasn't routinely here alone.

"I'll lock the doors as soon as you're gone. You won't be gone long, and I can start the clean-up."

"I just don't want to leave it another night." Claire cringed and pressed a hand to her ear. "It's getting worse."

I'd known it was worse than she was letting on when she'd taken two hours off today to go to a last-minute doctor's appointment.

"Go. You don't want your eardrum to burst."

Claire gave me a look that clearly said *can that happen?* I wasn't sure, but I motioned for her to leave anyway.

I turned the lock the instant the door swished shut behind her. This time of night, with very little traffic on the roads, the pharmacy was only ten minutes away. Claire would easily make it, and she'd be back in less than half an hour. I could get the floors done by then.

I grabbed the broom and set to work.

A cold draft hit my legs, and I stopped. Even if the central heating had died, it shouldn't be kicking out cold air. The draft seemed to be coming from the kitchen. Maybe we'd left the freezer open or one of us had accidentally bumped the thermostat from hot to cold?

I set the broom down and headed to the kitchen.

The back door hung open.

Sharp prickles ran down my sides. That door had been locked. There was no way the door opened accidentally.

I backed toward the door between the kitchen and the store front.

A blur of black flashed in my peripheral vision. I turned to run.

An arm snaked around my waist and another clamped under my chin. I didn't react fast enough to drop my chin the way Dan had taught me in our self-defense classes.

"If you scream," a man's voice said, "I'll kill you."

Not Jarrod's voice, Fear said, sounding a lot more logical than I felt. *It's not Jarrod.*

For all the good that did me. This man still had me. I'd been so naïve to think that, because we hadn't had any more trouble in the past two weeks, no one was watching the store. I'd started to think this was over and whoever it was had gotten what they wanted when Bob Jenner died.

I'd been naïve, convincing myself it was that way because I didn't want to think that, along with Jarrod still being after me, and having to testify in the trial for Janie's former teacher, I also had to worry about someone targeting my store.

My mind was rambling, but I couldn't seem to stop it. He'd said he'd kill me if I screamed. Did that mean he wasn't going to kill me? What was he going to do instead? Claire wouldn't be back soon enough to save me. The security cameras were recorded, but they weren't monitored. No one would have seen this man break in. Help wasn't coming.

And if Claire did come back in time to stop whatever he was here for, he might just hurt her too.

His arm tightened around my throat.

I had to focus and wait for my moment. Dan said part of self-defense was staying calm and picking the right moment. You usually only got one chance.

"What do you want?" I forced the words out.

His arm tensed. Pain, heavy and broad, enveloped my throat.

His head was by mine, but I didn't feel skin, only cloth. He must be wearing a mask. If he was wearing a mask, he didn't plan to kill me. Unless he knew about the security cameras and the mask was for their sake.

The smell of his cologne, something musky and cinnamon-sweet, threatened to choke me if his arm hadn't already been doing the job.

His arm tightened, and I couldn't get air. My lungs burned. My hands instinctively flew to his arm. I tugged at him. He didn't budge.

Then he eased off, and air rushed into my body again.

"Shut your business down." His voice was hard and gruff.

"Leave town." His arm tensed as if he were going to cut off my air again. "This is your only warning. Understand?"

I couldn't nod. I tried to say *yes* but my throat wouldn't work. I swallowed and finally got it out. "Yes."

"Good."

His arm let go, and he shoved me hard.

My forehead hit the counter, and I fell. The next thing I knew, I was on the floor.

My forehead felt like it was on fire, and something warm that had to be blood dripped down.

I was so stupid. If that had been Jarrod, I'd be dead and I'd have deserved it.

A small, more rational part of me knew that wasn't true, but it felt like it was. Dan was going to be angry.

And it was Dan I needed.

I eased my phone out of my pocket and dialed his number.

He answered on the first ring with, "Hey, Isabel."

"Someone attacked me."

DAN DABBED HYDROGEN PEROXIDE ON MY FOREHEAD. "IT'S NOT deep enough to need stitches."

He didn't say I was lucky. I appreciated that. I didn't feel lucky. I felt stupid. "I just didn't want Claire to miss her prescription."

Dan had called Claire on his way to me, redirecting her to go stay with Janie, who was already in bed. He'd left as soon as Claire got there. I'd stayed on the floor until he reached me. He'd helped me sit up, but wanted me to stay seated on the floor until he got a better look at my injuries.

"Bleeding's almost stopped now." He gently pressed the wound. "I probably would have agreed with you that you were safe for the few minutes it was going to take her. He must have been waiting for an opportunity."

Normally I would have nodded, but I couldn't move with Dan's hand on my forehead. He was sitting so close. All I wanted to do was lean into him and cry. But I couldn't.

"Was it…" Dan's voice was more hesitant than I'd ever heard it. "Do you think it was Jarrod?"

Thank God for small blessings. "It wasn't him. Wrong voice. Wrong height. Wrong smell."

Something flickered across Dan's face. "You're sure? If this was Jarrod, it's my fault for not providing you with protection sooner."

Dan shouldn't feel responsible for this at all. "It wasn't him." I rested a hand on the arm he wasn't using to tend my wound. "This guy told me to close my shop and leave town. Jarrod wouldn't want that. He'd want me where he could find me." My throat felt like I'd swallowed glass, but I forced myself to continue. "If this had been Jarrod, Claire would have come back to find the shop empty and me gone because he would have taken me."

Dan's breathing turned slightly ragged. He brought his free hand up and stroked a thumb across my cheek. Warmth spiraled through me.

We couldn't go there. I couldn't let us go there.

"This has to be related to everything else that's happened here." I blurted the words out, stumbling over some of them. "He wanted me to shut the business down."

Dan broke his gaze from mine and returned it to the wound on my forehead. He grabbed an adhesive gauze pad from the first aid kit. "Tell me again exactly what he said."

The words should have been seared into my mind, but my heart had been beating so fast that I'd felt light-headed, and I'd been more focused on survival. "That this was my only warning. I should close up shop and leave town."

Dan smoothed the edges of the bandage flat against my skin. "So we don't really know if his focus was on the shop or on your leaving. It could be that what he meant was, *lock up right now and go*."

I hadn't thought about it that way, but either part of the statement could have been the important part. And if what they wanted was for Claire and I to give up the store, why would they also want me to leave town? Unless it was a diversion?

I felt like I was running around in a maze.

"We also have to consider that he waited until Claire was

gone." Dan's voice had an edge to it. "They might have been targeting you alone rather than both of you."

If I'd been calmer, if I'd been thinking more clearly, I could have asked questions. But very few people would have that presence of mind when a man was choking them.

Assuming this was about me and that the important part was leaving town, I could think of only one person that would benefit. Janie's former teacher. She had a better chance of acquittal if I didn't show up in court. "This could be related to my testimony in the Glover case."

Dan's hands clenched. "I'll call DA Hall."

I leaned my head back against the island. All of it might have nothing to do with our shop. The spray painted message that we couldn't clearly read might have been a similar warning to the one I received tonight.

Bob Jenner might have been an unfortunate casualty. The person who killed him might have been waiting to threaten me. Or his death might have been meant to scare me away from town.

If that were the case, then even though I hadn't meant to hurt anyone, I was partly responsible for Scott losing his dad.

19

*D*an packed the supplies back into the first aid kit. "I still think you should go to the hospital."

I shook my head. Pain flared across my vision. "It's bad enough you're making me wait for an officer."

Dan gave me a long-suffering look. "We have to report this, especially if it might be related to the Glover case."

Intellectually, I knew that. It didn't make things any better knowing it. Especially given that the woman investigating the case didn't seem to like me much. "It's not Detective Austen coming, is it?"

Dan smirked. "No. She's off duty tonight. It's Zee. You remember him. He teaches the women's self-defense class."

Zee was one of Dan's closest friends. The man was also built like a military tank. I hadn't been able to take his class. His size alone had caused me panic attacks. But it'd be different to give him a statement across a table than to have him come into close contact with me the way he would have needed to in training.

Dan escorted me back to the front of the shop and pulled out a chair for me. "I'll make you a cup of coffee, okay?"

I smiled at him as well as I could. For some reason, my whole face ached. Probably from hitting the floor with it when I fell. "Okay."

While I waited for Zee, I needed to call Scott.

The background when he picked up was noisy—the kind of noisy that only happened in a crowded place. An automated announcement chimed, but I couldn't make out the words. Scott had said he wouldn't be in again until Monday. I hadn't thought to ask him why. At the time, it'd seemed intrusive. He didn't owe us an explanation. He didn't owe us work hours. He'd finally accepted some payment from us, but he was the one doing us a favor. We'd have struggled without the extra set of hands.

Once this was all over, I would take Flynn up on his request for employment. Claire and I had decided that, until then, we weren't comfortable with him coming in even at night.

"Where are you?" I asked. I felt a little like I needed to shout so Scott could hear me.

"Airport." His voice was raised as well, even though it was quiet on my end. "Saturday is my mom's fiftieth."

Right. He'd given far-away friends and family as the reason he was happy to work with us. Maybe I shouldn't tell him. He'd feel it was his responsibility to fix, the same as he had when he installed the security cameras after the vandalism. I'd never met Bob Jenner, but I could say one thing for him—he'd taught his son the value of responsibility and caring for others.

But I couldn't keep this from Scott either. He was—or soon would be—our landlord. He'd receive a copy of the police report once Zee filed it. Better he hear it from me. "Something happened tonight, but we have it under control."

I filled him in, downplaying the attack slightly.

"Are you and Claire alright?" There was a weird echo to his voice now, as if he'd gone into a restroom in the hope of hearing me better.

"For the most part. The police are here now."

He made a noise that was part groan and part growl. "When is this going to stop?"

I didn't have an answer for him. I wish I did, for all our sakes. "If you're thinking about canceling your trip, don't. You can't do anything here, and your mom's birthday is important."

I didn't have to say that we never knew how much time we'd get with the people we loved. He knew that as well as anyone after losing his dad.

Dan's voice and another man's floated to me from the kitchen. My body didn't instantly tense the way it normally did when I heard a strange man. The difference had to be Dan's presence.

Hypocrite, a tiny voice hissed at me inside my head.

If it wasn't Fear hassling me, it was my conscience. My insistence that Scott make the most of his time with those he loved rang a little false when I was ensuring Dan and I could never try a relationship. I had grounds to divorce Jarrod. He'd violated our marriage covenant in a way that we couldn't come back from. He'd beaten me to the point where he'd killed our unborn child.

But if you file for divorce, Fear chimed in, *he'll know exactly where you are.*

Once the trial date for Ms. Glover arrived, he'd know where I was anyway.

"Isabel?" Scott's voice jerked me back to the present. "Are you still there?"

"Sorry. I'm here." I almost blamed my head injury. I stopped myself just in time. That would only worry him and ensure that he canceled his trip.

"Get whatever you need to make the shop secure," Scott said. "New locks. Better locks. Add a lock. I'll reimburse you as soon as I get back, okay?"

That swelling feeling in my chest hit me again. The one that reminded me of how much I had to be grateful for. We could have gotten a landlord who didn't care about us. I'd heard stories about people whose toilets broke or whose heating went out in January and their landlords didn't show up for days. Mine let us make decisions and get things done in order to keep us protected.

"Thank you, Scott."

"No problem." His voice cracked slightly. "It's what my dad would have done."

20

I'd almost finished the edible cookie dough for my cookie dough icing when Dan's name and picture flashed on my cell phone screen. Ever since the attack last week, he'd taken to calling regularly while I was at work to see how I was doing. He didn't say so, but I suspected he was worried about PTSD. And that this invasion of a place where I should have felt safe might make me reconsider my decision to stay in Lakeshore permanently.

"I have good news or bad news depending on how you look at it," Dan said.

At this point, I couldn't take any more bad news. "Spin it so it sounds good."

Dan chuckled. "I never thought I'd hear you ask for sugar-coating. At least, not on anything other than a cupcake."

Normally that would have gotten a laugh from me as well. I

hadn't felt much like laughing for the past few days. It was hard to stay positive when so many people wanted me to disappear, one way or another.

"Devon Glover, Ms. Glover's brother, has been vocal on his social media accounts about the 'supposed witness' the police have. He's made a lot of slurs about what kind of person you must be. Suggesting the police paid you or that you have some other motive for wanting revenge on his sister."

A tight feeling ran all the way down my torso. Hearing that some man I didn't even know was trying to harm my reputation made me feel small and unsafe again.

What he said shouldn't have mattered. He didn't even know me. We'd never meet.

Maybe my reaction was about what I'd gone through with Jarrod. But this felt different. More...normal. As if maybe this was what anyone would feel, not like an overreaction because I was me.

"That's the sugar-coated version?"

"I don't actually think there is a sugar-coated version."

"Go on, then. I'm not sitting down, but I can take it."

"When I told DA Hall what happened to you, she was suspicious that it could be a case of attempted witness intimidation. You don't have any social media accounts, so Devon couldn't harass you or mobilize his followers to cyberbully you."

Wouldn't that be ironic if hiding from Jarrod had actually

benefited me? Sort of. "So her theory is that he escalated to stalking me in person?"

"That's the theory, yes."

I stuck a spoonful of cookie dough into my mouth. It didn't bring me the comfort I was looking for. Instead, it stuck in my throat, the sweetness suddenly cloying.

Dan's end of the call was quiet, as if he were giving me a minute to process what he'd said. If criminal behavior could be genetically inherited, then the Glovers both got the gene.

Except that it couldn't. Which meant that their sociopathy must be caused by the way they were raised. What kind of home life would have resulted in a sister who hurt children and a brother who would threaten an innocent woman to save his guilty sister.

"They don't have any solid evidence that it was him, though?"

Dan sighed. "Unfortunately, not. Scott had the security company forward the recordings to the station, but your attacker wore a mask. The height and build is similar, but that's not enough to press charges on."

I eyed the bowl of edible cookie dough. If I didn't need it, I'd be tempted to find a corner and curl up to eat the whole thing.

Food had never made me feel better, though. It'd always been the therapeutic act of preparing food that soothed my mind. Maybe it was time to work on that salted caramel cupcake I'd been thinking about.

First, I had to face this problem. Ignoring it wouldn't make it less real. "You did say there was some good news, right?"

"I did. But it depends on whether you'll feel comfortable doing it or not."

Something in the tone of Dan's voice made me think he'd acted as my defender, protecting my right to choose whether to be a part of this plan. That meant it'd be hard. And scary.

"What's the idea?"

"DA Hall would like to stage an 'accidental' meeting between you and Devon Glover. We'll ask him to come to the station for something, and you'll already be in the waiting room. Detective Austen and I will be in plain clothes in the waiting room as well. The idea is to see if he seems to recognize you, and to give you a chance to hear his voice."

In other words, they wanted to set up an ambush. They might catch a break, and Devon would show surprise or anger when he saw me. He might even ask what I was doing there. Either of those would be the ideal situation. If not, my memory was the back-up plan. I would remember my attacker's voice, and his smell, for a long time.

I could see now why Dan said he had good news or bad news depending on how I looked at it. The good news was we had a new lead on who might have killed Bob Jenner, vandalized the store, and threatened me. The bad news was I'd have to face that new suspect if we wanted to be able to prove he'd had anything to do with it.

I might be a coward in many ways, but I'd long ago decided I wouldn't allow a murderer to walk around free if I could help prevent it.

"I'll do it."

I ARRIVED AT THE POLICE STATION AN HOUR BEFORE DEVON Glover had been told to arrive so that Detective Austen could give me a long list of things I wasn't supposed to say or do. Don't bring up the Glover case. Don't ask him directly whether he'd attacked me.

At first, I gave her an *I'm not stupid* eyebrow raise. By the end, I gave up and just nodded.

Looking at the positive side, coming to the police station and speaking with the police was becoming easier each time I did it. I'd never be as comfortable as my friend Nicole was with stopping by the local police station, but at least I didn't expect every officer to turn me over to Jarrod anymore.

Though, the clothes Austen and Dan wore probably helped. Dan wore mismatched clothes with tattered hems and holes that showed the layer beneath. He hadn't shaved, and his face had dirt smeared across it. He also smelled like he'd used beer as a cologne.

Austen had aged herself. Instead of the pant suit she'd been wearing the first time I met her, she'd put on a floor-length, shapeless peach-toned dress covered in paisleys. She'd pinned her hair up under a gray wig, and someone had applied make-up to her face in such a way that her eyes looked sunken and her skin looked weathered.

I probably wouldn't have walked past Dan on the street without recognizing him because of how close we were. I definitely would have overlooked Detective Austen, though.

Austen glanced at the clock on the wall. "Show time."

Dan stumbled out into the waiting room first, playing his part the second we left the interview room. The transformation was so complete that I wouldn't have known he wasn't homeless—and I'd interacted closely with the homeless population in the last town I'd stayed in before coming to Lakeshore.

Dan signaled that Devon Glover hadn't arrived yet. Austen and I took our seats.

I pulled out my phone and pretended to read. That seemed like a more natural way to be when he came in rather than staring at the door waiting for him.

The entry door swished open, and a man stepped inside.

He matched the social media profile picture that Dan and Detective Austen showed me. Average height. Average build. Just like the man who'd attacked me.

None of his features said *murderer*. They all said *average guy*. He had a normal-sized straight nose, eyes that weren't shrunken or shifty, and a slightly weak chin.

He gave his name to the desk clerk and turned toward the room.

His gaze slid over Austen, then past Dan. His nose twitched slightly as if he could imagine how unpleasant sitting anywhere near Dan would be. His gaze stopped on me, but his expression didn't change. He seemed more like a man who was trying to decide the best spot to sit, and I looked the least problematic.

He picked a seat two down from me, using me as a buffer between him and the other two.

I was now supposed to engage him in conversation to see if I recognized his voice. "Excuse me?"

The words came out a lot more hesitantly than I'd expected. My heart felt like it was beating in my throat rather than down in my chest where it belonged.

He didn't look in my direction, as if he thought I must be speaking to someone else.

"Excuse me?" I said, forcing my voice to be louder than I was normally comfortable speaking. "Did you notice if any of the cars out front had parking tickets? It seems ridiculous that the only parking spaces they have for the public are out front, and they're metered, don't you think?"

Austen shot me a quick *stay with the script* glare.

Devon Glover finally looked in my direction. "Which car was yours?"

An uncomfortable tingle ran down my neck and down my back. His voice was close to that of the man who attacked me, but it wasn't identical. The problem was that meant he might have tried to disguise his voice when he broke in to threaten me. Whoever had broken in had taken the time to find a ski mask to wear. It wasn't a stretch to believe he might have thought about his voice as well.

He was looking at me with his eyebrows slightly raised.

"The one out front," I blurted.

Technically all the spots were "out front." Since I didn't know the make and model of the cars out there, I couldn't even pretend one was mine. Dan had parked in the back parking lot reserved for officers' cars.

Devon Glover's forehead tightened in the way that it did for people who couldn't lift a single eyebrow at a time but only two together. "Which one out front?"

"The little one." I sounded like only half my brain was working. Maybe I should have stuck with Austen's idea of commenting on the weather, but that'd seemed forced. Very few people would strike up a conversation about the weather while in a police station.

Devon huffed out a breath and leaned back in his chair with his arms crossed over his chest. "Well, I didn't see any tickets on the cars out there if that helps."

His voice was so similar to what I'd heard, and yet different enough that I couldn't say for sure that it'd been him. Maybe if we'd been able to trick him into saying the exact words my attacker had without him knowing what we were doing. If he knew what we were doing, he'd disguise his voice more. Or maybe if my attacker had said more. But neither of those were going to happen. One of the reasons Dan and Detective Austen chose to have this staged meeting between us was so Devon would be less likely to know and try to hide his voice. That didn't help if he'd chosen to disguise his voice during the attack, though.

He stuck his feet out in front of him.

Red speckles covered the tops of his shoes. My pulse kicked up so high that I could feel it in my throat.

The red spots weren't the right color for old blood. Old blood would have had a brownish quality to it. And after all the steps my attacker took, I couldn't imagine he'd be stupid enough to wear blood-covered shoes to the police station.

These spots were brighter, almost orange, like the spray paint across our windows. There weren't many spots, and they were faint. Had he not called attention to his feet by sticking them out, I wouldn't have seen them. Any detective who interviewed him wouldn't have been able to see them either, since his lower half would have been hidden by the table.

I shifted in my seat as if I were bored and antsy about waiting so long for my turn. I wanted to clue Dan and Detective Austen in on what I'd seen.

I nodded toward Detective Austen's feet. They were swathed in the kind of slip-on orthopedic shoes favored by the elderly.

"Are your shoes comfortable? I do a lot of walking, and I'm looking for a new pair."

Devon made a noise from the other side of me as if he thought I was an overly-talkative person who couldn't stand to sit in silence.

Detective Austen's expression said she also clearly thought I'd lost my mind.

But Dan slid sideways onto the seats. To anyone who didn't know what he was doing, it would have looked like he was a homeless drunk preparing to take a nap where he could get one.

But I saw his gaze go directly to Devon Glover's shoes.

"o you really want to make that icing with brown sugar?" Claire asked.

I glanced down at my measuring cup. I had almost poured brown sugar into my Swiss meringue buttercream. Maybe it would have still worked, but it wasn't a way I'd ever tried before.

Claire took the measuring cup out of my hand and poured the sugar back into the proper container. "I burnt myself this morning because I forgot to put on an oven mitt."

I took the measuring cup back from her, scooped out the granulated sugar, and added it to my egg whites. "Okay..."

Claire gave a you're-smarter-than-this sigh. "Why don't you call Dan and ask him about that Glover woman's brother? That way we can keep from damaging ourselves or our business because we're distracted."

I'd avoided calling Dan and pestering him. I didn't want to be the kind of person who couldn't wait patiently for someone else to do their job.

"He said he'd call if they made an arrest."

I turned on the mixer to drown out any more arguments from Claire. Maybe I was being obstinate for no reason. If Dan didn't have answers, he'd simply say he didn't have answers yet.

My reticence made no sense in the present. It was just that every time I reached for the phone to call Dan, I remembered how Jarrod hadn't wanted me to call him. He'd called me clingy and needy, even if I had an urgent situation.

My meringue formed stiff peaks. I dropped in my butter piece by piece.

Dan wasn't Jarrod. Dan was nothing like Jarrod. I had to keep reminding myself of that so that the things that had happened to me in the past didn't unintentionally affect my relationships in the present.

Still, shouldn't I trust Dan to call me when the time was right? My knowledge of even friendships was so limited that navigating the lines made my head hurt like I'd eaten something too cold and given myself a brain freeze.

My Swiss meringue buttercream turned silky. I'd always been a fan of traditional American buttercream. I even liked the little crust it formed over time. But Swiss meringue buttercream tended to be more popular among customers.

I shut the mixer off.

"Finally." Claire held up her phone. Dan's contact information was on the screen. She tapped it and then hit the speaker button. "If you won't call him, I will. I want to know if we have to keep acting like we're kids on a field trip who are supposed to stay with their buddy."

An image of Claire and I strolling everywhere with our hands linked and tiny backpacks on our backs flashed into my mind. I grinned.

Claire scowled at me.

"Holmes," Dan's voice said from the other side of the phone. He clearly hadn't checked his screen before answering.

"It's me," Claire said. "And Isabel. We're hoping for an update."

Of course she'd say *we*.

"I was just about to call, so your timing is good."

Claire shot me an I-told-you-so look.

I pursed my lips at her.

"You'll be happy to know that we arrested Devon Glover for vandalism. His fingerprints matched the hand print officers took off your glass. We were also able to check his credit card records, and we found a purchase he made from a paint store the day before. Forensics are working on matching the paint from his shoes with the sample scraped off your window, but since he confessed, it's semantics at this point."

"He confessed to everything." Claire's voice was almost a screech.

"To the vandalism only." Dan's tone held a resignation that

made my stomach clench. "Once we presented him with the evidence against him, he admitted to spray painting *keep your mouth shut* on your windows in an attempt to intimidate Isabel."

Keep your mouth shut made a lot more sense than the garbled message we thought had been written there. If this was Devon's first attempt at spray painting a message, it was no wonder his words had been about as legible as a kindergartener's first attempt at writing their name.

"He says he'd have no reason to kill someone," Dan said. "His words were 'I'm not a killer. You're trying to frame me like you framed my sister. All I did was spray some paint.'"

Claire made a grumbling noise.

Tension pooled in my forehead, and I rubbed the line across the top of my eyebrows. "That's not exactly reassuring considering I know his sister is guilty of both murder and attempted murder of more than one person, including me."

Dan made a confirmatory sound. "Detective Austen and DA Hall agree with you. They think it's too much of a stretch to believe two separate people were targeting the store. They have him on the vandalism, but he's also being charged with murder, assault, and breaking and entering."

The assault would have been against me.

Claire grinned in a way that would have put a Cheshire cat to shame. "That makes the most sense. Devon Glover must have been waiting in the store to ambush Isabel. Mr. Jenner showed up first, tried to take the gun away from him, and Glover killed him accidentally."

Dan and Claire said something else, but my mind tuned it out. If that were what had happened, it would certainly explain everything in a neat and tidy way. Scott would have closure. Claire and I could be safe in our business again.

I should feel the same sense of relief that Claire was radiating. I'd been the one to spot the paint on his shoes, after all.

But his voice hadn't been a perfect match, and he hadn't smelled the same.

"Does this mean they won't be investigating anyone else?"

"Of course they won't," Claire said before Dan could answer. "They have the person who did this. Right, Dan?"

"That is the situation at present. The investigation is considered closed."

---

22

*T*he first thing I did once we disconnected with Dan was go to my office and call Scott.

Detective Austen would place an official call to him now that they'd arrested someone for his father's murder. She might have already done so.

But, in a small way, this was my fault. His father died because someone wanted to hurt me. I needed to apologize to him. Hopefully he wouldn't be the kind of person who would loath the sight of me so much now that he'd want us out of the building.

That was a risk I had to take. Despite my reservations, the police and DA Hall were sure Devon Glover was behind all of this. That meant I'd played a part, however unintentional.

Intentions mattered, but pain wasn't erased simply because someone didn't intend to cause it. If I wanted to be able to continue liking myself even a little, I'd need to make things right with Scott.

The call rang twice. Three times. I pulled the phone away from my face to hang up before his voice mail picked up. He'd see my number on his phone and call back. This wasn't something I wanted to leave with a machine.

"Hello?" Scott's breathless voice came through the line.

I mashed the phone back to my ear. "Has Detective Austen called you?"

"About an hour ago."

Dan must have waited to call us until after the official notification had been made to the family.

The rattle that came with wind across a phone speaker filled Scott's end of the line and then passed. "Sorry if there's background noise. I went out for a run afterward to clear my head."

"I use baking the same way." Putting this off wouldn't make it any easier. "I wanted to apologize to you."

There was a sound on Scott's side like footsteps on gravel. He must have started walking again. "For what?"

For what? I would have expected him to either acquit me or tell me it'd take him awhile before he could stand to speak to me again. I hadn't expected him to seem to not even know what I was talking about.

"For the part I played in all of this."

The whoosh of a car and more footsteps but no words.

"Scott?"

"I think you need to start from the beginning. How, exactly, did you play a part in this?"

Shoot. He must think I meant I'd been arrested too as an accomplice. "The man who killed your father was there to hurt me. Didn't Detective Austen tell you that?"

"No." The pause before he spoke was long enough that it made me think he'd shaken his head, only to realize belatedly that I couldn't see him. "All she told me was that they'd charged someone for the murder of my dad, as well as for the vandalism to the shop and the attack on you."

Maybe not giving the victim's family details was standard procedure. I wasn't sure. Jarrod had liked to tell me about all the ways he interrogated suspects. He never talked to me about the victims or their families. Maybe that should have been a clue to his real character had I been paying attention early enough.

"The words spray painted on the windows were *keep your mouth shut*. I witnessed an attempted murder in the spring, and I'm supposed to testify in December. The man they arrested for your father's murder is the brother of the woman I'm testifying against. They think he was waiting for me, your dad stumbled across him, and he ended up collateral damage."

"That doesn't make sense."

Had I not explained it clearly enough? It was possible I'd jumbled my words because I wanted to get it all out. "What part? I'll go over it again."

"Not what you said. What the police believe. What did that woman's brother achieve by killing my dad?"

I didn't have a psychology degree, so I didn't know if it was normal for a person to have to move through the stages of grieving multiple times. This sure sounded like the denial stage, though. Maybe once Scott accepted that they'd found his father's killer, he'd have to fully accept that his father was gone. That would be a hard step. The least I could do was walk through it with him.

"He didn't go there intending to kill him. He went there intending to scare me into leaving town. Your dad must have gotten there before Claire and I, got into a struggle of some sort with him, and was shot accidentally."

"Yeah, here's the thing. He didn't leave you a message."

The bell on the front door jingled, signaling customers entering. I slipped from my chair and closed the door. This was the kind of conversation that definitely needed to stay private.

"He left a message in spray paint on the window."

"Like a week later." Scott's voice had gotten louder and more animated. "How were you supposed to know that my dad's death was a message for you. He should have written *leave town, Isabel* in his blood or something."

A shudder ran through my arms. Thank goodness he hadn't. I might have actually done it, despite my promise to Dan.

"Do you see what I'm saying?" Scott continued. "If my dad's murder was connected to this other case, the killer didn't gain anything if he didn't make it clear. He had the perfect opportunity to scare you away. He'd killed once, and you would be next if you didn't do what he wanted. But he didn't tell you what he wanted. That message I washed off the window was too little, too late."

Scott's theory had a certain amount of logic to it. The vandalism hadn't been random. Devon Glover had taken the time to try to write a specific message—to tell me what he wanted me to do. He wanted me to keep my mouth shut.

Which wasn't even the same message as the man who attacked me. The man who attacked me wanted me to close the shop and leave town.

"So you think we're dealing with two different people?"

"The patterns are too different for it to be the same people, don't you think?" Scott's breathing picked up, as if he were power walking now to get back home or back to his car. "The one thing we know the brother did was very hands off. He came in the night and wrote a message. That's deescalating."

He had a point. Someone who killed might then physically accost another person. But why downgrade to a spray-painted message, then go back up again?

"The police aren't investigating the case anymore. They think they have the right person."

A car beeped in response to a key fob, and then a door opened and closed on Scott's end. The background noises died out. "What about Claire's cousin who's the cop?"

Dan had only been involved recently because it seemed like the present-day case had a connection to the past case. His involvement wasn't even official since Dan's family members had been the ones killed and almost killed by Ms. Glover. He'd been kept in the loop only as a courtesy, and of course, because he'd been the one to convince me to testify. I didn't have any sort of leverage with the Detective who was actually in charge of the case—a Detective Labreck.

I certainly didn't have any influence with Detective Austen.

"It's not his case."

"Could you see if there's anything he can do to convince someone to reopen the case?"

"I'll ask him."

An engine roared to life on Scott's end. "Call me back right after."

I disconnected the call with Scott and peeked out my office door. A couple and a singleton with a computer sat at the tables. Three people stood in line, but Claire seemed to have it under control.

I wasn't technically supposed to be out front anyway. Claire had taken one look at the gash across my forehead and decided we didn't need the kind of rumors that would circulate if customers saw my face in this condition.

I was all prep work today and preparing orders for pick-up. That could all wait.

I closed the door again and dialed Dan's number.

As soon as he picked up, I explained Scott's theory. "Detective Austen didn't even tell him Devon Glover's connection to me. Do you think there's any chance of convincing Detective Austen and DA Hall that they've got the wrong guy?"

"First of all, we don't know if he is the wrong guy." Dan's voice had that *let's slow down and take a breath* tone.

I flopped down into my chair. "Sometimes your calm nature can be infuriating."

The words were out before I realized I was going to say them. My body tensed instinctively. I shouldn't have said that. I shouldn't have—

"So Claire has told me many times." Dan sounded like he was trying not to laugh for fear of aggravating me more.

What he didn't sound was angry or insulted. In fact, he almost sounded...happy that I'd told him he was frustrating at times.

Something snapped into place in my brain. No, he didn't sound happy because he frustrated me. He sounded happy that I felt free enough—safe enough—to tell him.

In the past, when I'd felt frustrated with him or upset, I'd backed away. This time, it'd just come out.

"I can tell you more of your flaws later if you'd like." I put a smile into my voice, so he'd know I was teasing.

"Only if you let me tell you all your good qualities in return."

I wasn't sure I was at a place yet where I could believe any of the things he might say, but it felt like I'd come one step closer. "I'd like a raincheck on that."

"Anytime. As for the case," Dan's voice sobered, "I don't think there's any chance of Hall or Austen re-opening the investigation unless we have a more convincing suspect to present to them. Especially since we brought them the idea of this being related to the Glover case in the first place. Right now, all the focus is on strengthening the case against Devon Glover for when it goes to trial."

I could see that. If we went to them now and said we'd made a mistake or didn't believe he was the one, we'd look like we were trying to cause trouble. "I did tell Detective Austen that I couldn't be sure the voice matched."

"She's working under the belief that he tried to disguise his voice."

Which I'd also considered. Austen was doing her job and doing it well. She had brushed it off, though, when I said he didn't smell the same. She'd chocked it up to cologne or a new laundry detergent.

"I'll see what I can do," Dan said, "but this isn't my case, and my caseload is heavy right now."

Scott and I couldn't ask Dan to neglect the cases he was supposed to be investigating in order to undermine another detective's work. Not only would that cause friction within the department, but it'd also mean those other families who depended on him didn't get the help they needed.

"I'll text you if Scott or I can think of anything or anyone else."

We disconnected the call.

Maybe Scott and I were tilting at windmills like Don Quixote and his hallucinations. My dad used to always use Don Quixote as an example to me when I came up with crazy stories to explain something simple as a child. He'd said there was nothing wrong with imagination as long as we were able to remember where the line between fantasy and truth lay.

Scott could be, as I first suspected, unable to accept this because accepting it meant accepting his dad was gone. I didn't have that problem, but I did know that being on high alert felt more normal to me than being happy and at peace. Even in the moments when I was sitting around watching a movie with Dan and Janie, I'd sometimes tense, my body anticipating pain despite the situation. Maybe I was still subconsciously more comfortable being in danger. Not that I wanted to be in that state, but that it was the state of least resistance for me after it being the status quo for so long.

I redialed Scott. "There's nothing Dan can do unless we have a better option for them."

"I might have that. Do you remember that my lawyer was supposed to set up an appointment with Edwardo Sharp, the man who'd asked about buying the property?"

That hadn't been long ago, but it felt like it had. "I actually had forgotten with everything else that'd happened."

"That meeting is set up for tonight. I might as well keep it. If Edwardo Sharp seems suspicious at all, it could give support to our theory."

I guess it was our theory now. Scott had proposed it, but he'd mostly convinced me. At the very least, I wanted to help Scott find the closure he needed. If I hadn't indirectly caused his father's death, I'd also sleep better at night.

"What's you plan?" I asked.

"I've done enough business deals with my dad when I was apprenticing in the summers. I know what a prospective buyer should act like and the questions he should ask. If he seems off, we can ask Claire's cousin to at least run his name through the system. If everything is normal, all I've lost is a couple of hours of my time."

The plan was sound. There really was nothing to lose. "Just be careful okay. Don't make him suspicious that you think he's anything other than a buyer in case you're right."

"Yes, Mom." Scott's tone said he was teasing rather than actually annoyed at my protectiveness. "And Isabel?"

"Yes?"

"Even if it turns out Devon Glover did kill my dad while waiting for you, you have nothing to apologize for. You're doing the right thing testifying. You're not responsible for the choices anyone else makes, no matter how much someone tries to make you feel like you are or no matter how much you second guess yourself."

My throat felt like the air was once again being choked out of me. He was talking about the situation with Devon Glover and his dad, but he might as well have been talking about my relationship with Jarrod. He'd always blamed me when he hurt me. If I hadn't made him angry, he wouldn't have hit me. If I'd taken better care of the house or met his needs better. If I'd only been different.

Scott's words shone back into all of that and cut away the fog. Intellectually, I'd always known I wasn't to blame for what Jarrod did, but my heart had a harder time believing it. Scott's words made it feel a little truer for my heart.

Even though it was inadequate, all I could think to say was, "Thank you."

23

"Watch this, Isabel!" Janie called.

I turned from where I'd been helping Dan wash up the dinner dishes.

Janie stood inside the kitchen door, holding the cat toy we'd picked up for Pirate when I got her from school. The toy was a garishly colored bird, complete with florescent feathers, attached to a stick by a long string.

Pirate crouched at Janie's feet, tail twitching and his gaze laser-beamed onto the toy. Considering Pirate spent most of his time napping next to Janie as she played, seeing him even follow the toy into the kitchen was a success in itself. The vet had told Dan and Janie at Pirate's most recent check-up that he needed to lose some weight, and so far nothing had motivated Pirate to abandon his favorite activity—sleeping.

Janie twirled the toy in the air in a weird spastic imitation of flight. Pirate wiggled his bottom and then launched himself into the air, almost reaching the height of Janie's shoulders.

She swung the toy again. "We did two laps of the living room before this too."

I gave her a high five. "Way to go. Dr. Gerry will be proud at Pirate's next check-up."

"We're going to do more laps."

She took off into the living room again. Pirate raced behind her.

I turned back to the dishes, but Dan had stopped washing and was looking at me. His expression was soft, like he would have been happy to watch Janie and me for hours.

"She asked me yesterday why you live with Claire rather than with us."

I glanced back at the door Janie had exited through. She'd been asking a lot more questions lately. The last one was how I was related to them. Apparently most of the people she spent time with outside of school were part of their huge extended family.

This new question felt more challenging than that. I picked up the dish cloth I'd been using to dry the dishes and twisted it around in my hands. "What did you tell her?"

"That you couldn't live with us because we aren't married."

Dan shifted back to the sink and plunged his hands back into the water. I moved to his side.

He let the words hang in the air as if he wanted to put it out there as an idea for me to think about. Like he wanted me to know he'd thought about the future and what might happen between us if I filed for divorce from Jarrod.

We hadn't dated. We hadn't kissed. Thinking about a permanent future with Dan probably should have seemed strange given those things, but it didn't. It felt like the thing I'd want the most if I were free.

I wouldn't have thought I'd consider remarrying, even if I had found a way to gain my freedom from Jarrod and didn't have to always be afraid of him. I wouldn't have thought I'd ever be brave enough to try again.

But standing next to Dan at the sink, drying while he washed, listening to Janie play in the other room, I could picture it. I could see us as a real family.

My eyes burned, and I blinked fast.

I wasn't free. And if I tried, Jarrod would kill me. If he thought Dan was anything more than a casual friend, if he thought Dan knew the truth, he'd probably kill him too. Where would Janie be then? Assuming she didn't end up a pawn in Jarrod's plan to punish me.

I couldn't risk that. I wouldn't risk that.

My phone vibrated from where I'd left it on the table after clearing away the dishes.

Scott's name flashed on my screen.

I slid my finger across the screen to answer.

"Did you change the locks like we talked about?" Scott asked.

Shoot. I should have told him, but the locksmith hadn't sent me an invoice yet. "We did. Each door has a fresh lock and a dead bolt now. I haven't sent you the bill yet because I haven't received it."

"Don't worry about that. Send it along as soon as you receive it." Scott's voice was strange, overly casual and light. "Right now, I need you to bring me a set of keys. I'm about to show the property, and I forgot that the locks were changed."

That explained his weird tone. It was his professional voice. I was used to normal, casual Scott.

He was probably also embarrassed. Whether Edwardo Sharp was his father's killer or not, Scott's young looks combined with him not having the key undermined him.

"I'll bring you copies right away."

"Thanks. I'll be waiting at the bakery."

I didn't have time to make another set of keys. That would be asking them to wait another half an hour at least as I drove to a hardware store and had them copied. I'd give Scott my set and make a copy of Claire's keys tomorrow.

I turned back to Dan and explained the situation to him, leaving out the part where Scott was showing the building to a potential murderer. Leaving out the part where Scott was showing the building at all. Dan would ask why, out of concern for Claire and I losing the shop, and that would lead back to the potential murderer part. Dan wouldn't approve of Scott's choice, but it was Scott's choice.

Besides, Scott wasn't going to confront the man or do anything suspicious, and he wouldn't be there alone. He'd have a real estate agent with him.

I grabbed my purse and drove to the shop. Scott stood out front, but he was alone.

I climbed out of my car. "Where's Edwardo Sharp?"

Scott stamped his feet and blew out a breath that turned white as soon as it hit the cold evening air. "I got here early, so I could open the place up."

His voice had that same forced light tone to it. I'd been wrong before. It wasn't his professional tone at all. He was nervous.

I would have been too. Even though this was a potentially normal situation, it was also a tense one. He might be meeting face-to-face with the man who killed his father.

I unlocked the first lock, switched keys, and unlocked the dead bolt. The alarm system beeped, and I typed in the code. "Take a couple deep breathes."

Scott nodded. He stepped inside. Even though his breath wasn't creating white clouds anymore, his chest rose and fell deeply.

"I didn't expect to be this nervous," he said.

"Keep these, and I'll make another set." I slid the two keys off my key ring and handed them to him. "Shouldn't the real estate agent be here already?"

Scott slid the keys into his pocket. "What real estate agent?"

My throat spasmed. Had I misunderstood? "You were planning to show the place alone?"

Scott continued his deep breathing. "Of course."

Oh no. That was a bad idea on so many levels. I lowered my voice even though we were alone. "If this man killed your father, you can't be here with him alone. He might try to kill you as well."

"Why would he do that? If he wanted to buy this building, and I look like I'm going to sell it, he has no motive."

I wanted to rub my hands over my face, but I kept them at my sides. "We can't be sure that was the only motive."

Scott turned a shade of milky gray, and his breathing kicked up again. "I just assumed...I didn't think..."

"I'll stay, okay?" The words were out before I had a chance to question them. I couldn't leave him here. If something happened to him, I'd never forgive myself for abandoning him. If there were two of us, we had a much better chance of staying safe.

Scott nodded. A bit of color came back into his cheeks.

The bell above the door jingled. "I hope I'm not early."

Cold darted through my veins, stiffening all my limbs.

I knew that voice. It was the same one that hissed threats into my ear while choking me.

"Not at all." Scott's voice was light and confident now. He sounded the same as he had when he was playacting for Claire and me when we first met. "I've asked the tenant to join us. She knows the property better than I do at this point."

Run, Fear screamed in my head.

Pull yourself together, my rational self demanded.

I'd known this was a possibility. That was the whole plan after all. I just hadn't thought through the implications of staying. I guess I hadn't been totally convinced that Devon Glover wasn't the one who'd attacked me. Part of me thought Devon was the guy.

I was sure now. Comparing this voice with Devon's voice left no question.

I couldn't let on. I pasted my Jarrod-smile on my face, the one that even a trained FBI agent hadn't been able to see through.

I turned, but I didn't extend my hand to shake his the way Scott would have. Every self-preservation panic neuron in my body was firing. If he touched me, I might lose my control. "I was happy to help out." I dialed my smile up a notch until it was at full intensity. "I'm hoping you'll continue letting us rent the place." I cocked my head to the side even though my stiff neck protested. "At the same rate, of course."

"I wouldn't dream of evicting good tenants." Sharp's voice had a natural growl to it.

I forced my vision to focus. We might need to give a description of him to the police afterward. Edwardo Sharp might not even be his real name.

The man was handsome in a hard-wrought way. Dark hair. Dark eyes. Unsmiling lips. A tattoo peeked out from the collar of his suit and another from the cuff of his sleeve. Even his body looked solid under his suit jacket.

The way he looked at me said he'd noticed that I hadn't offered to shake hands.

A tremor started in my fingers and worked its way up my arms. Should I offer to shake now or would that seem more suspicious?

"The location isn't big," Scott said, "but let me give you the tour."

"No need." Edwardo slithered his gaze from me to Scott. "I'm ready to close the deal now."

There was the slightest hesitation as Scott turned away from the door he'd been about to head through and back around to face Edwardo. He glanced in my direction. He'd figured it out too.

"I'd feel better if I showed you the whole property first," Scott said. "That way there's no chance that you'll end up saddled with something you didn't bargain for."

I had to give it to him. His tone revealed nothing. His dad or his degree trained him well to stay professional. The only clue was that tiny stutter to his step and the eye shift in my direction. Hopefully, Scott didn't do anything more than that. Edwardo gave me the sense that he'd pick up on it.

"If you insist," Edwardo said.

He moved past me, and his scent hit me like a shove. Even if

I hadn't been sure about his voice, I'd remember that musky note.

As soon as they went into the kitchen, I'd duck into my office and call 9-1-1. I couldn't go outside without the bell attached to the door giving it away and making Edwardo suspicious.

"But perhaps Isabel will join us on the tour," Edwardo said, "since she knows the most about the building."

He gestured with his arm for me to proceed him into the kitchen. I forced my legs to carry me.

Had I told him my name? I was sure neither Scott nor I had mentioned it. Scott had referred to me as *the current tenant*, and I didn't his hand so I hadn't introduced myself.

If there was any doubt left in my mind, it was gone now.

The way Edwardo watched me let me know he'd done it on purpose.

We were playing a game now. Who would call the other's bluff first.

It wouldn't be me. He didn't know that I'd been through worse than simple intimidation. If I played this game long enough, he might be forced to leave. He could have killed me before, which meant he didn't want to leave a trail of any more bodies if he could help it. He was smart enough to know that the more people he killed, the more likely he was to be caught.

I walked as casually as possible into the kitchen and gave the slowest, most in-depth tour that I could—just like I would if I actually wanted Edwardo to buy the building.

Finally, I ran out of things to say.

Edwardo pulled a sheaf of papers out of his breast pocket. "I went to the liberty of having my lawyer draw up a purchase agreement. You'll see that I'm actually offering more than what your lawyer stated the asking price would be."

He pointed the paper toward the front of the shop, like an air traffic controller directing a plane. Scott and I both followed the non-verbal instruction.

We went to the table Edwardo indicated.

He spread out the purchase agreement.

We'd been right that he'd killed Bob Jenner because he'd refused to sell this shop. But why? It wasn't like this was a good place to cook meth or whatever the current drug of choice was. Maybe he wanted to use the shop as a front for laundering money? That made only marginally more sense. He wouldn't have needed this particular shop. There had to be cheaper, easier to acquire shops all along this street.

Whatever the case, he certainly had no intention of allowing Claire and I to go on with business as usual once he owned the shop. He'd either evict us or try to force us into joining his scheme.

Scott was reading over the purchase agreement, running his finger along each row of words slowly, as if he had a reading disability. He was probably trying to buy time to figure out what to do.

Scott lifted his head and flattened his hand on top of the

paperwork. "Your offer is more than fair, but we're not done showing the property, and we expect multiple offers on it."

He slid the papers back across the table toward Edwardo.

Edwardo smiled. His lips went out more than up, and the smile never reached his eyes. "I guarantee you that my offer will be better than what you'll receive anywhere else."

Scott climbed to his feet. He fumbled the chair slightly. It tipped backward, and he caught it. "You'll have your chance to put in an offer. Now, as much as I hate to cut this short, we have another prospective buyer arriving soon."

Scott met Edwardo's gaze as if there was nothing wrong.

Edwardo nodded, walked to the door, and turned the deadbolt.

24

*S*cott jerked beside me like he had strings attached to him and someone gave them a tug. "What are you doing?"

Edwardo faced us both. He eased aside his suit jacket. A gun hung at his waist. "Stopping this charade. Are you going to sell me this building and walk out of here alive or do I need to negotiate in a different way?"

His hand brushed against the butt of his gun.

"Is that the same deal you offered my dad?" All the professional veneer had cracked off of Scott's voice. His words wobbled.

Edwardo only smiled. Not an admission of guilt that could be used against him if we happened to get out of this alive. But certainly not a denial either.

My body wanted me to become small. To hide. Scott's body had clearly pumped adrenaline through his system, making him blurt out what he was feeling without thinking it through.

Not that anything we did would matter now. Edwardo wasn't going to allow us to leave alive, regardless of whether Scott signed the purchase agreement or not. If he let us go, he had to know that we'd head straight to the police department. A contract signed under duress wasn't binding.

The only way he got this building was if Scott signed the paperwork and then Edwardo killed him.

And me since I was a witness.

I had zero bargaining chips. He held all the cards here. He had a gun. He could kill us and escape, just as he'd done when he killed Bob Jenner. Maybe he didn't know about the security cameras? Those could identify him.

"This building is monitored. If you kill us, the police will know it was you."

His top lip pulled back slightly. "Security cameras are only as good as the servers the recordings are housed on. Those servers should have been upgraded long ago. Old wiring can catch fire easily, and then the whole building will be lost. Very unfortunate."

Of course, if he had enough money to buy this whole building for well above market value, he had enough money to pay someone to burn down a building. Perhaps he even kept someone on retainer for that sort of job. Edwardo had no qualms about killing people. He certainly wouldn't balk at arson, even if that resulted in the death of an employee who ended up trapped in the building as it burned.

The thought made me shudder.

Edwardo had clearly come here with a plan for what to do if Scott wouldn't sell him the building immediately. He didn't seem like someone who left loose ends. Scott's life might have met an "accidental" end even if he had signed those papers.

He'd even kept his back to the windows once locking the door, using his body to shield his gun from the big front windows. No one walking by outside would see anything unusual about three people in a bakery. I'd have to make a wild gesture that Edwardo wouldn't be able to miss in order to signal anyone who happened by that something was wrong.

We had to get out of here. I just had no idea how yet. Maybe if I could get a knife from the kitchen. It seemed like I'd fall into the cliché of "never bring a knife to a gun fight" if I did that, but it was better than nothing. If he didn't notice it, maybe I could place it at his neck while he was distracted by the papers.

He wasn't likely to leave me alone in the kitchen, not with a door in there and the chance that I'd call the police. But if I could use my back as a blocker, I might be able to manage it.

The knowledge that this was so different from how I would have handled this situation a year ago flashed across my mind.

Either attempts on my life by strangers had become so common that my brain approached it with the same detachment that it had when it'd kept me alive while living with Jarrod or Dan's self-defense training had a bigger impact than I realized.

I edged back a step. "Why don't I get us something to eat?"

Scott raised his eyebrows at me, his eyes wide, as if my brain had completely malfunctioned.

Edwardo smiled in a way that lifted only half his mouth. "I'm no amateur. Even if I went with you, I know that sharp objects are kept in kitchens." He pulled his gun and used it to direct Scott back to the table where we'd been sitting before. He stopped me before I could join him. "Now baby Jenner, are you going to sign those papers or do I need to show you what a bullet will do to your friend's knee caps? We can easily step into her office for the show so that we don't have any peepers outside spoiling the fun."

Scott's gaze bounced from the gun to me to the papers. His skin looked like he'd rolled around in chalk dust.

His hand reached for the pen.

"Don't." The word came out instinctively.

Scott froze, and his upper body shifted to face me. His expression clearly said *you want me to let him shoot you?*

"He's not going to let us go, especially if he shoots me. We've seen his face." I glared at Edwardo. Meekness and subterfuge hadn't worked. Maybe gutsiness would. After all, it wasn't like he could kill me twice. He wasn't the first real-life villain I'd faced. I'd slept next to one for years. "No mask this time."

For the first time, Edwardo's smile reached his eyes. It sent a frigid jolt through my core. "I wasn't certain you recognized me." He sighed and swept the papers off the table. "I don't really need to waste my money on this building anyway since you've both decided to be stubborn. I'll give you one more chance to cooperate. Ms. Addington, call your new friend Flynn and tell him to meet you down here. Without giving anything away."

Flynn? If he wanted me to call Flynn, then Flynn must have been right. The events at the bakery were connected to his drug dealer. Edwardo must either be that dealer or have been hired by him. We were in bigger trouble than I'd even thought. Based on Dan's assessment of Flynn's dealer, he'd have no problem murdering us. And Flynn.

But why bring Flynn down here? And why did he want to buy this property? That didn't fit with anything Flynn had told me about the situation or any of the theories we came up with for why his dealer might be targeting the bakery.

"And why should she do what you tell her if you're going to kill us anyway?" Scott asked.

Edwardo's eyes narrowed a fraction as if he couldn't wait to be rid of us. "Because death doesn't have to be quick. A person can live for hours with broken bones and missing teeth. You can bleed out slowly, one small cut at a time, or I can do this compassionately with a head shot. It's your choice."

Scott swiveled to the side and vomited. Bile burned the back of my throat, but I couldn't tell if it was from the sound and smell of Scott losing his dinner or if it was because we were going to die here tonight unless I could figure something out.

At least if I called Flynn, I might be able to tip him off somehow without Edwardo realizing what I was doing.

Dear God, I prayed silently. *Give me wisdom.*

"I'll call him," I said. "May I reach into my purse and take out my phone?"

"Slowly."

I set my purse on the table so that he could see everything I was doing. We didn't need him shooting us accidentally because he thought I was reaching for a weapon. Not that I didn't have pepper spray in my purse. I did. But he could pull the trigger on his gun faster than I could dig it out and aim, even if I was close enough to have the spray hit him.

I gingerly pulled my phone from my purse, scrolled through my contacts, and dialed the Wendts' number. I didn't have anything else for contacting Flynn.

Mr. Wendt answered the phone rather than Flynn. "Isabel!" He drew the first part of my name out as if it started with three E's. "When are you coming by with more cupcakes?"

I had to keep my voice steady so as not to make Edwardo angry. I had to avoid him insisting I put the phone on speaker.

"I was hoping you'd come to the store next. I'd like you to see what I've done with it."

Edwardo made a speed-it-up motion with his hands and mouthed the words "No inviting anyone else."

A rush of heat and then cold flooded my body like I had the flu. I hadn't considered that Mr. Wendt might come with Flynn tonight. If Flynn didn't figure out that something was wrong, I'd be responsible for getting Mr. Wendt killed too.

"But that'll have to be another day." I shot the words out so quickly that it was a miracle I didn't garble them. "I need to talk to Flynn."

"To Flynn?" Mr. Wendt's voice shifted slightly, in that way parents had when they suspected their children of a crush.

I wanted to cover my eyes. Let's add mortification to fear for my life. "Flynn asked me about a job, and I wanted to get him started."

"Oh." The excitement in Mr. Wendt's voice shot so high Edwardo could probably hear it. "Yes. Let me get him."

He must have moved the phone away from his face, but his voice calling Flynn's name still carried out of the phone. I almost moved the phone away from my ear.

I couldn't risk that Flynn was a loud phone talker like his dad. If he got suspicious about anything I said, he'd give me away. I gently touched the button on the side of my phone to turn the volume down.

Flynn's voice greeted me next. "I didn't think you'd actually give me a call about a job."

I had planned to after we solved Bob Jenner's murder. We were so busy that we wouldn't be able to keep the pace we were setting much longer, even with Scott. My throat tightened. If

Scott and I died here tonight, Claire would never recover. She almost hadn't made it through the murder of a perfect stranger a few months ago.

Hiring Flynn ever was out of the question now. His involvement with Edwardo made him unsafe.

Maybe that wasn't fair, though. Edwardo wouldn't have me luring Flynn down here if he and Flynn were associates.

"Yeah, I need a hand. Tonight. The stove isn't working again."

"You've tried the valve?"

I had to do something to make this conversation seem less normal to Flynn. Even if I could, him considering it odd enough to call the police was a long shot. Unfortunately, it seemed like our only shot.

"Yeah, you did such a great job of fixing it before. I guess I should have watched more closely. But I'd really appreciate it if you could pop down tonight."

"I can come, sure. I thought you were closed Mondays. What are you even doing there?"

His tone had gone hesitant. We both knew Flynn hadn't come to fix the stove before. The question was whether that would be enough to tip him off that I was in danger or if he'd simply think I was drunk dialing him.

"We are closed on Mondays, but you know how it is when you're running your own business." I had to give him another clue that something was wrong. One might not be enough. "I know it's late, so I'll throw in a box of blueberry muffins. You and your dad seemed to enjoy those last time I visited."

He might think I'd just gotten them confused with someone else I'd visited. I needed something else.

"Did you leave any for your mom?" I asked.

Edwardo eyes tightened around the edges. "End it." He mouthed the words so softly I knew Flynn wouldn't have been able to hear it. I barely could. "Now."

I acknowledged him with a small nod. "Anyway, I'll be waiting. Knock on the door because it's locked, and remember to bring your tools."

Edwardo snatched the phone from my hand and hit the end button himself.

My ending had been a bit sloppy. There was no way that Flynn was going to understand "the door is locked" was code for "I'm being held hostage" and "bring your tools" meant "bring help."

But maybe he'd at least know something was wrong. Maybe, just maybe, it would be enough.

Edwardo motioned for me to join Scott. "Now we wait."

Scott had his head down on his arms, a small pile of paper napkins he'd used to clean his face crumpled up next to him. The stench of his lost stomach contents made my stomach clench again.

Scott didn't even look up when I sat in the chair beside him. His reaction was probably the normal one. My mind was clear now. It wouldn't stay that way. Not if past experience was any indicator. Hopefully Dan wouldn't have to peel a weapon from my in-shock hands the way he had the last time. Though, if he did, that would at least mean I'd managed to get the gun away from Edwardo.

Tackling Edwardo and fighting him for the gun seemed unnecessarily risky. He was bigger, and he'd be expecting me to do something. He could shoot me and then Scott.

No, what I needed to do now was stall and pray Flynn caught my plea for help.

Stall because Edwardo might not think he needed to keep us alive now that I'd called Flynn. Scott's body language clearly said he'd given up hope.

I needed to plant a different idea in Edwardo's head. "So now we're leverage against Flynn for whatever reason you had me lure him down here?"

Edwardo pulled another chair around so that he could see both the front windows and us, while keeping his gun on a side where it wouldn't be spotted by anyone outside.

"Something like that," he said.

Scott moaned softly beside me. An instinct to comfort him rose up inside me. I rubbed his back in soft circles the way I would Janie's back. In many ways, Scott was still just a kid.

That was probably why I'd been able to hold myself together so long. My life wasn't the only one at stake.

"Could you at least do us the courtesy of telling us why you were trying to buy this place? Why you tried to scare us away? Why you just had me trick Flynn Wendt into coming down here?"

I prayed that Flynn wouldn't come alone. Whatever he'd gotten himself into, I still didn't want him dead.

Edwardo shifted in his chair, leaning back so that he seemed to take up more space. "Flynn managed to collect some very condemning evidence against me before he went away. Evidence of our business dealings together, conveniently scrubbed of his involvement. I knew something was wrong when he pled guilty to possession. Flynn never sampled the merchandise."

My body felt like it belonged to someone else. That's why Mr. Wendt and Flynn's legitimate employer hadn't noticed his drug habit. He didn't have one. He'd simply confessed to having one so that the police wouldn't investigate further when he was caught with drugs.

Keep going, my rational self urged. *Keep him talking.*

"And you think he hid it here?"

"I know he did. I replaced the decrepit Mr. Wendt's cleaning lady with one of my own. She searched their house twice over. I rented out the apartment Flynn used to live in and stripped it as well. The only other place where he could have hidden it was here. He never expected his father to give up the family business while he was inside."

That explained why Flynn had been so helpful. He hadn't wanted to work for me or watch for known associates of a drug dealer. He wanted an opportunity to retrieve whatever he'd hidden here. When I visited, he'd realized Edwardo was trying to get his hands on the evidence. Since Flynn hadn't turned the evidence over to Edwardo, he must have been trying to black-mail his former associate with it.

Poor Mr. Wendt. This was going to break his heart.

Everything that had happened was about getting that evidence.

"Why kill Bob Jenner?"

Scott flinched under my touch.

"He caught me trying to strip this place to find Flynn's stash." Edwardo spoke calmly as if he were explaining how he'd found a parking spot on a busy street. "The place was supposed to be unoccupied. When Jenner came strolling in and caught me, he left me no choice. He told me to stay where I was, that he was calling the police."

He'd accidentally forced Edwardo's hand so that Edwardo couldn't just tie him up and continue searching. Once Edwardo shot him, he must have realized the police would arrive soon. He'd had to abort his search.

He hadn't been able to get back in after that. First, the police had the scene cordoned off, and then, as soon as they released it,

Claire and I found the vandalism. Scott had a security system installed right away. The only time it wasn't on was when the bakery was also full of people. That left Flynn without a way to sneak the evidence out and Edwardo without a way to gain access to the store for a long enough time period to search it.

A faint click came from the kitchen. I stayed as still as possible. It'd sounded like the new deadbolt. If it was, help was here. Flynn didn't have a key to come in the back. He must have called the police, and they got Claire's set.

Edwardo didn't turn his head in that direction. He hadn't heard it.

I needed to be ready to take Scott and I to the ground, out of the line of fire. I also needed to keep Edwardo distracted. If he heard anything suspicious, he could easily shoot us first.

"That was very unethical of Flynn." I pitched my voice high and loud, as if I were outraged. "He had evidence against you, and he didn't take it to the police. I have no patience for black-mailers. They're the lowest of the low."

I rambled out everything I could. It meant I couldn't hear when the exterior door into the kitchen swished open, but hopefully Edwardo couldn't either.

I just kept talking.

The door to the kitchen burst open with shouts of "drop your weapon."

I shoved Scott to the side. We both toppled down. A gun boomed. Then multiple shots and shattering glass.

"Suspect down," one of the officers said. "Send an ambulance to our location."

He had to be talking into a radio. My field of vision narrowed down, and my head felt light. It was over.

"Isabel." Scott's voice was reedy. "Can you get off of me please? I think I landed in my own vomit."

25

*S*cott and I sat next to each other on the tailgate of one of the ambulances, wrapped in blankets. I'd have to ask Dan later why they gave blankets to people who might be in shock.

Scott sat hunched over, his elbows on his knees. He wore a sweatshirt that was two sizes too big for him. He had, in fact, been covered in his own vomit. One of the paramedics had given him a shirt, so he could change. We weren't steady enough to leave immediately, and Scott had looked almost more trauma-tized about being covered in puke than about being held at gunpoint.

"I'd be dead now if it weren't for you," Scott said, not sitting up. "How did you stay so calm?"

Edwardo hadn't touched me, held me down, or restrained me in any way, for starters. Last time I'd faced down a man with a gun, I'd had to wrestle him for it. It hadn't gone as well. I didn't remember much of what happened after I got the gun away from him. One minute I was telling him and his girlfriend to stay put, and the next minute Dan was there taking the gun out of my hands.

More than the absence of touch, though, I'd been thinking about Scott. I'd wanted to protect him. Panicking felt like a luxury. I hadn't had a problem touching his back when he was afraid because he'd needed my help.

But no young man wanted to hear that. He already admitted I'd been the one to get us out alive. I didn't want to emasculate him by saying I stayed calm for his sake.

Besides, it wouldn't have been the whole truth. As much as I hated to admit it, life with Jarrod had prepared me for facing down people who wanted to hurt me. I'd had to stay calm no matter what Jarrod did or said because that was the only way to stay alive.

I put a hand on Scott's back. "My husband used to beat me. Not a lot is scarier than that."

Scott bobbed his head as if I hadn't just revealed something awful about my past. His passive acceptance pointed to him being in shock, even if I wasn't. Or maybe I was. My abusive past wasn't something I generally revealed, but Scott and I had gone through a terrible situation together.

"I want to make the same deal with you that my dad made," Scott said.

He stated the words bluntly, as if we'd been discussing that instead of what happened to us. That alone made me reticent to take him up on the offer.

"You shouldn't make any major decisions right now."

Scott raised his gaze. "I didn't make it now. I made it weeks ago. I was waiting until all this was resolved to tell you. I like the bakery. It's relaxing. I want to be a part of it."

That was unexpected. I'd thought that if Scott gave us the same deal, he'd be doing it out of a sense of loyalty to his dad's memory, not because we somehow won him over. "You want to keep working a couple shifts even once the estate is sorted?"

Scott nodded. His gaze seemed to snag on something beyond me, and he wedged his hands between his knees and leaned over as if he wasn't sure whether he needed to throw up again or not.

I swiveled around until I could see what he'd seen. A man who had to be the medical examiner, based on his lack of a uniform, walked beside a gurney. A black body bag rested on top of it.

I hugged the blanket tighter around me. Edwardo must not have followed the officer's order to put down his weapon. The whole thing took place so fast that I hadn't been paying attention to all the words being yelled.

When the S.W.A.T. officer ushered Scott and I from the building and over to paramedics, I hadn't looked in Edwardo's direction. I hadn't wanted to see where the shots fired landed. One of the paramedics who checked Scott and I over had said the lead officer had taken a bullet to his vest. So if Edwardo fired first, the officers would have had to open fire in return.

At least it was over.

Behind the stretcher, Flynn sat in the back of a police cruiser. I hadn't been able to talk to him and thank him for calling the police. Maybe I didn't have to. He had been the one to hide evidence that could convict a criminal in his father's bakery to begin with. But he also hadn't needed to go to the police after my weird phone call. He had to know when he did that the questions they'd ask could eventually lead to his arrest for withholding evidence.

Detective Austen stood near the back of the cruiser, talking to a tall man with dark hair. Not any man. Dan. Claire must have called him after the police came for her keys.

He spun around. Had I called his name? Scott had lifted his head and was looking around, so I must have.

I hadn't felt shaky or weak at all, but now tremors started in my feet and rushed up my body until I felt like I couldn't have moved if I wanted to. My eyes burned, and I blinked against the pressure.

Dan swept me up from my sitting position into his arms, and I clung onto him. I didn't realize I was crying until his jacket felt wet under my cheek. It was like my brain had locked everything up until I saw Dan and knew for sure I was safe.

"You're okay," he whispered into my hair. "You're okay."

I wasn't sure which one of us he was reassuring.

I eased back from him. Scott inched over on the back of the ambulance and patted the spot beside him. I sat down. Dan took the small space beside me, his arm pressed up against mine.

"What will happen to Flynn?" I asked.

It sounded more gracious than I felt. If I were being honest, I didn't much care where Flynn ended up. I did care about Mr. Wendt and what finding out what his son had done would do to him. Thank goodness he had his daughter to lean on.

"He's cut a deal," Dan said. "The evidence he had on Edgar Serranno also implicated a lot of other people in his organization that the police have been trying to convict for years. Flynn showed them where it was in exchange for immunity."

"Edgar Serranno?" Scott's voice still sounded a bit spacey, but it was closer to his normal tone than it had been before.

"Flynn's drug dealer," I said. "Sort of." Since it turned out Flynn had been a business partner rather than a client, I wasn't sure how to refer to Serranno anymore. If it turned out that Flynn had been working out of his father's bakery, Mr. Wendt was going to have a hard time recovering any sort of trust in his son.

Dan leaned around me slightly, so he could see Scott as well. He inclined his head toward the body bag. "The man you knew as Edwardo Sharp was actually Edgar Serranno. Apparently, he and Flynn had a falling out, and Flynn started collecting information that he could use to blackmail Serranno. Before he could use it, he was caught with some of the drugs he'd planned to include in his stash as evidence. He confessed to possession in order to protect his bigger project."

And we'd all ended up caught up in it because Flynn stashed his "project" in the bakery. "Where was it?"

"Under a floorboard in the office."

Dan brought me up to my feet. He took the blanket off my shoulders, folded it, and left it in the ambulance. "Time to go home. Claire will have paced a path in the carpet by now."

"Vacuumed a path more like."

Dan chuckled, but he linked his fingers with mine as if he couldn't blame Claire, even if her way of dealing with stress was a bit odd.

Scott got up and folded his blanket as well.

"Do you need a ride home?" Dan asked.

Scott shook his head. "I'm okay to drive now, and I'd rather not leave my car here. With how things have gone lately, I'd come back in the morning to find it'd been towed or stolen."

Scott headed in one direction, and we headed in the other. We passed by the body bag where Edwardo Sharpe—Edgar Serranno lay.

It'd once seemed like the only way to stay safe was to hide from Jarrod, but I hadn't been safe recently. In truth, the only way to stay completely safe was to not live, to hide in my house and never leave. And even then, I couldn't protect myself from a heart attack or a stroke. I couldn't guarantee a single minute of my life. Only God could.

So maybe it was time.

Maybe it was time to try to free myself from Jarrod once and for all.

Dan opened the car door for me, but I held up a *wait* hand. I dug the card for the divorce lawyer he'd given me a few months ago out of the inside pocket where I'd kept it. The edges were frayed, and one corner was bent.

I handed it back to him.

He looked down at it. "Does this mean you've decided not to file for divorce?"

His voice didn't give anything away, but his Adam's apple bobbed up and down.

"I've decided not to use that lawyer. I have a different one in mind."

In the previous murder case I'd gotten wrapped up in, I'd called Kirkland Law Offices. The receptionist had turned out to be the lawyer's wife, and she'd shown me care and sympathy when she thought I was in a bad situation. If I was going to risk this, I wanted her and her husband by my side.

The corners of Dan's eyes crinkled.

I shrugged. "Jarrod's going to find me one day. If not because I file for divorce then because he shows up at the Glover trial. I decided I'd rather he find out my location on my terms."

Dan brushed the hair back from my face. "To show him you're not afraid of him anymore?"

That wasn't possible. Unfortunately, I'd always be afraid of

Jarrod. He was like an old wound that would always ache when the weather changed.

I'd just made a decision about how I'd react to that wound. "To show him that I'm not going to let him or my fear control me anymore."

LETTER FROM THE AUTHOR

Only one book left in the Cupcake Truck Mysteries!

I hope you enjoyed watching Isabel take another step forward. The choices she made in this book were challenging ones for her.

In the final book, Jarrod returns. If you're like me, you've been waiting for it and also dreading it.

If you want to know when the final Cupcake Truck mystery releases, make sure to sign up for my newsletter at www.subscribepage.com/cupcakes.

And if you enjoyed this book, I'd really appreciate it if you'd leave an honest review on Amazon or Goodreads. Reviews help fellow readers know if this is a book they might enjoy. Even a short sentence helps!

Love,

Emily

P.S. Signing up for my newsletter also means you'll get advanced sneak peeks at the new series I'll be releasing later this year.

RECIPE: LEMON "MERINGUE" PIE CUPCAKES

One of the first cupcakes Isabel bakes in her new bakery is her lemon meringue pie cupcakes. These aren't topped with actual meringue. Instead, they're made with a silky Swiss meringue buttercream. These are one of my personal favorites because I love the contrast of the tart lemon with the sweet frosting.

To make the buttercream, you will need a stand mixer for this one. If you don't have a stand mixer, or you don't want to go to the trouble of making a Swiss meringue buttercream, I'll also give you instructions at the end for how to top these with a traditional meringue instead. (I've made them both ways, and they're equally delicious. If you make the traditional meringue, just be aware that you need to eat them more quickly.)

INGREDIENTS

Cupcake:

1 1/2 cups all-purpose flour

2 teaspoons baking powder

1/2 teaspoon salt

1/2 cup unsalted butter, softened

1 cup granulated sugar

2 large eggs, at room temperature

1 1/2 teaspoons vanilla extract

1/2 cup 2% milk, at room temperature

2 medium lemons, zested and juiced

Lemon Curd:

1/2 cup fresh lemon juice

2 teaspoons lemon zest

1/2 cup granulated sugar

3 large eggs

6 tablespoons unsalted butter, cut into pieces

Swiss Meringue Buttercream:

1/4 cup pasteurized egg whites*

2 cups powdered sugar

dash of salt

3/4 cup unsalted butter, softened

2 teaspoons vanilla extract

*This actually works better with egg whites separated from whole eggs, but I understand that many people aren't comfortable with that option. If you are okay with using raw egg whites, you'll need the whites from 2 large eggs.

INSTRUCTIONS

1. Preheat oven to 350 degrees F, and line a muffin pan with cupcake liners.

To Make the Cupcakes:

2. In a medium bowl, whisk together flour, baking powder, and salt. Set aside. These are your dry ingredients.

3. In a large bowl, use the high speed on your mixer to beat together the butter and sugar for about 2 minutes, until smooth and fluffy.

4. Turn the mixer down to medium-high, and add the eggs and vanilla. Beat until combined. It should look smooth.

5. By hand, gently mix your dry ingredients into your wet ingredients until just combined. Do not over-mix.

6. In a small bowl, mix together milk, lemon juice, and lemon zest.

7. Immediately but slowly add the milk mixture into the batter. Mix gently. You want them to be combined but not overmixed.

8. Use the batter to fill the cupcake liners 2/3 full.

9. Bake for 16-18 minutes or until a toothpick inserted into the center comes out clean.

10. Cool completely on a wire rack.

To Make the Curd:

11. In a heavy saucepan, whisk together lemon juice, lemon zest, sugar, and eggs.

12. Turn the heat on to medium-low and add the butter. Whisk until curd is thick enough to make tracks and you see the first couple of bubbles. This should take about 6 minutes.

13. Remove from heat. Run the curd through a strainer into a bowl to remove any bits of egg that might have overcooked.

14. Lay a sheet of plastic wrap on the surface of the curd to prevent a skin from forming, and chill in the refrigerator for at least 1 hour.

To Make the Buttercream:

15. In the bowl of your stand mixer, on low speed, mix together egg whites, powdered sugar, and salt until sugar is fully moistened.

16. Turn off the mixer and scrape down the sides.

17. On the medium speed of the mixer, beat the mixture for another 5 minutes.

18. Reduce the mixer speed to medium-low.

19. Add the softened butter 1 tablespoon at a time. Allow

each chunk of butter to be fully incorporated before you add another.

20. Mix in the vanilla extract.

21. Scrape down the sides of the mixer again.

22. Return the mixer to medium speed and beat the icing for 10 more minutes.

To Assemble Cupcakes:

23. Cut a small hole out of the center of each cupcake.

24. Fill the hole with 1 teaspoon of lemon curd.

25. Pipe the buttercream onto the top of the cupcakes.

Makes 12-16 cupcakes.

TRADITIONAL MERINGUE OPTION

3 eggs whites

1/2 cup granulated sugar

1. In a medium bowl, beat the egg whites until they begin to gain volume.

2. Slowly add in sugar while continuing to beat.

3. Whip until stiff peaks form.

4. Pile the meringue onto the cupcakes. Use the back of a spoon to create peaks.

5. Toast the meringue with a culinary torch.

MAPLE SYRUP MYSTERIES

Looking for something to read until the next Cupcake Truck Mystery comes out? Try Emily James' Maple Syrup Mysteries. This thirteen book series is complete and available in both print and ebook formats. The first four books are also available as audiobooks.

Criminal defense attorney Nicole Fitzhenry-Dawes thought that moving to the small Michigan tourist town of Fair Haven and taking over her uncle's maple syrup farm would keep her far away from murderers, liars, and criminals. She couldn't have been more wrong...

If you love small-town settings, quirky characters, and a dollop of romance, then you'll enjoy this amateur sleuth mystery series.

Pick up the whole series at https://smarturl.it/maplesyrupmysteries.

ABOUT THE AUTHOR

Emily James grew up watching TV shows like *Matlock*, *Monk*, and *Murder She Wrote*. (It's pure coincidence that they all begin with an M.) It was no surprise to anyone when she turned into a mystery writer.

Alongside being a writer, she's also a wife, an animal lover, and a new artist. She likes coffee and painting and drinking coffee while painting. She also enjoys cooking. She tries not to do that while painting because, well, you shouldn't eat paint.

Emily and her husband share their home with a blue Great Dane, a Boxer-mix, eight cats (all rescues), and a budgie (who is both the littlest and the loudest).

If you'd like to know as soon as Emily's next mystery releases, please join her newsletter list at www. subscribepage.com/cupcakes.

She loves hearing from readers.